Dear parents, caregivers, and educators:

If you want to get your child excited about reading, you've come to the right place! Ready-to-Read *GRAPHICS* is the perfect launchpad for emerging graphic novel readers.

All Ready-to-Read *GRAPHICS* books include the following:

- ★ **A how-to guide to reading graphic novels for first-time readers**

- ★ **Easy-to-follow panels to support reading comprehension**

- ★ **Accessible vocabulary to build your child's reading confidence**

- ★ **Compelling stories that star your child's favorite characters**

- ★ **Fresh, engaging illustrations that provide context and promote visual literacy**

Wherever your child may be on their reading journey, Ready-to-Read *GRAPHICS* will make them giggle, gasp, and want to keep reading more.

Blast off on this starry adventure . . . a universe of graphic novel reading awaits!

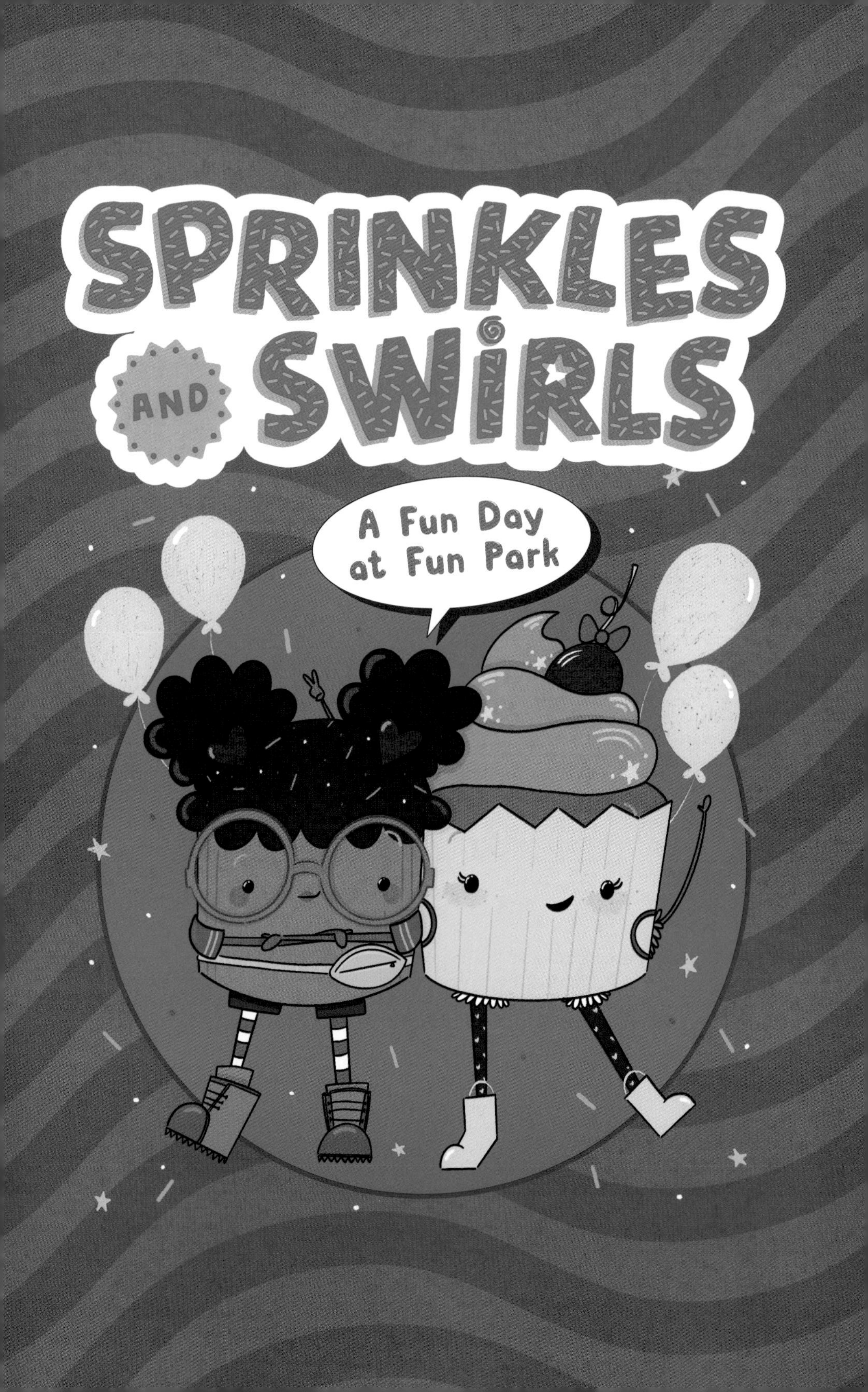
SPRINKLES AND SWIRLS
A Fun Day at Fun Park

For Lennon, the happiest cupcake of all! –L. S.

For Kramer, Sadie Lou, Baby Ben, Christy, and Gabrielle–
thank you for everything! –S. A.

SIMON SPOTLIGHT
An imprint of Simon & Schuster Children's Publishing Division
1230 Avenue of the Americas, New York, New York 10020
This Simon Spotlight edition December 2021
Text copyright © 2021 by Lola Schaefer
Illustrations copyright © 2021 by Savannah Allen
SIMON SPOTLIGHT, READY-TO-READ, and colophon are registered trademarks of
Simon & Schuster, Inc.
For information about special discounts for bulk purchases, please contact Simon & Schuster Special
Sales at 1-866-506-1949 or business@simonandschuster.com.
Manufactured in the United States of America 1021 LAK
2 4 6 8 10 9 7 5 3 1
Cataloging-in-Publication Data for this title is available from the Library of Congress.
ISBN 978-1-6659-0329-5 (hc)
ISBN 978-1-6659-0328-8 (pbk)
ISBN 978-1-6659-0330-1 (ebook)

SPRINKLES AND SWIRLS

A Fun Day at Fun Park

Written by **LOLA M. SCHAEFER** ★ Illustrated by **SAVANNAH ALLEN**

Ready-to-Read *GRAPHICS*

Simon Spotlight
New York London Toronto Sydney New Delhi

HOW TO READ THIS BOOK

Sprinkles and Swirls are here to give you some tips on reading this book.

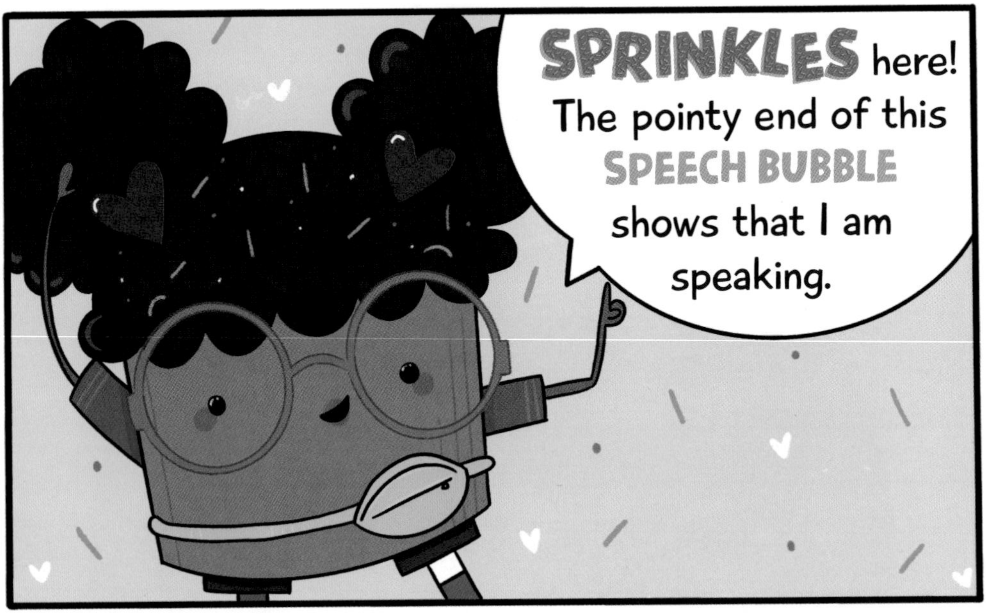
SPRINKLES here! The pointy end of this SPEECH BUBBLE shows that I am speaking.

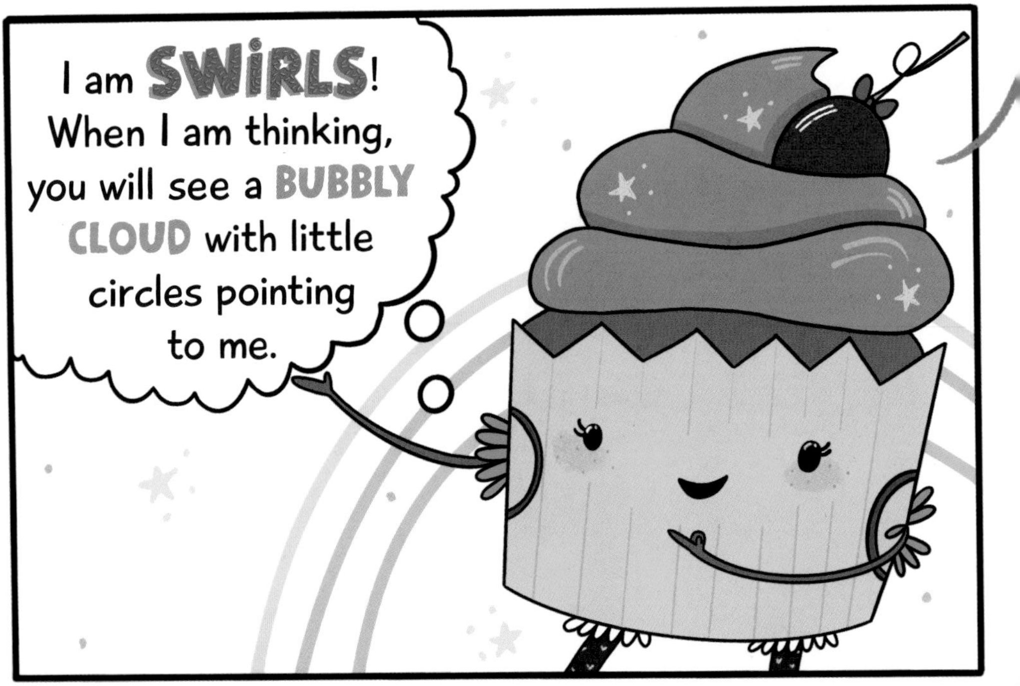
I am SWIRLS! When I am thinking, you will see a BUBBLY CLOUD with little circles pointing to me.

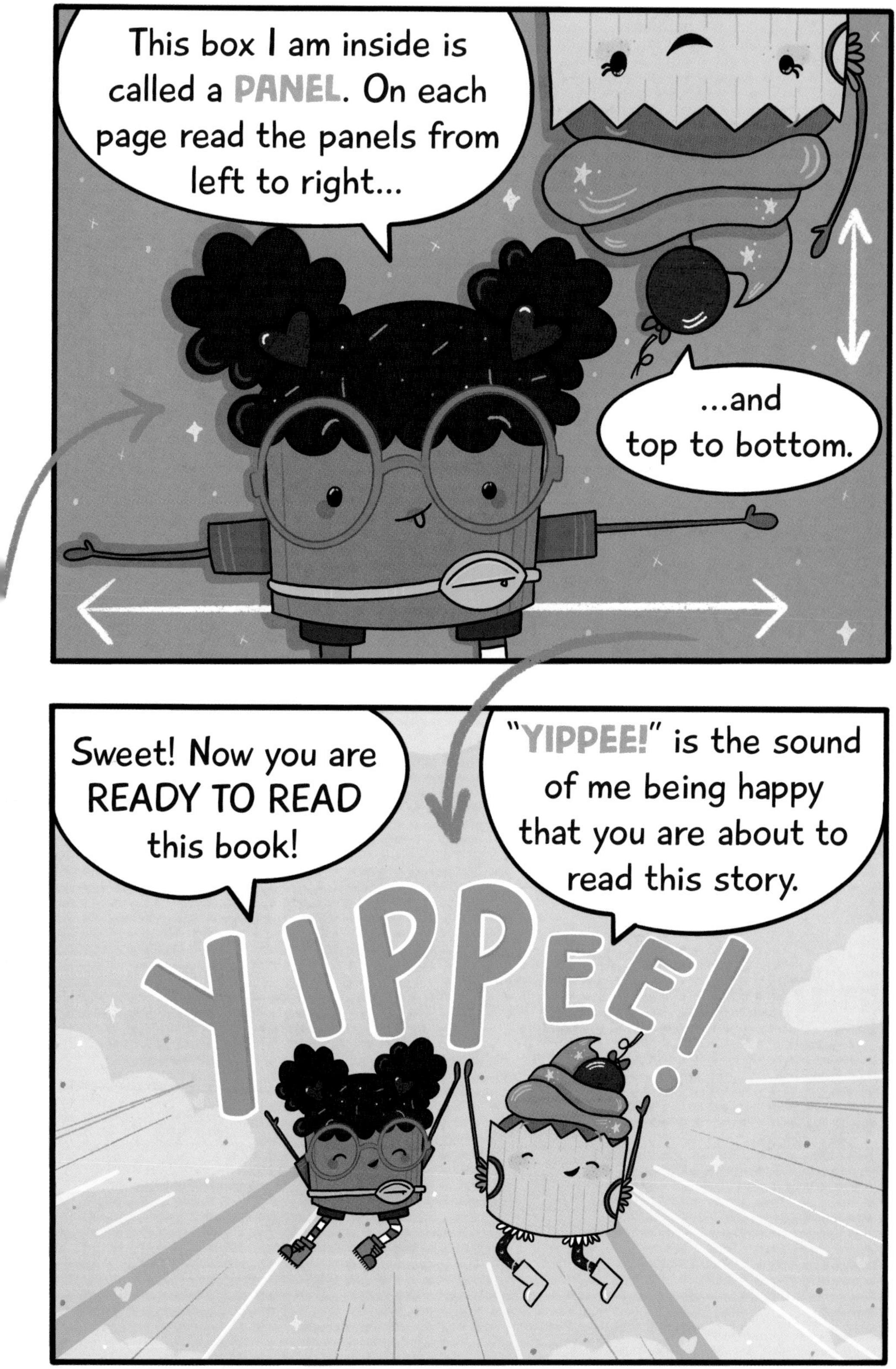
This box I am inside is called a PANEL. On each page read the panels from left to right...
...and top to bottom.
Sweet! Now you are READY TO READ this book!
"YIPPEE!" is the sound of me being happy that you are about to read this story.
YIPPEE!

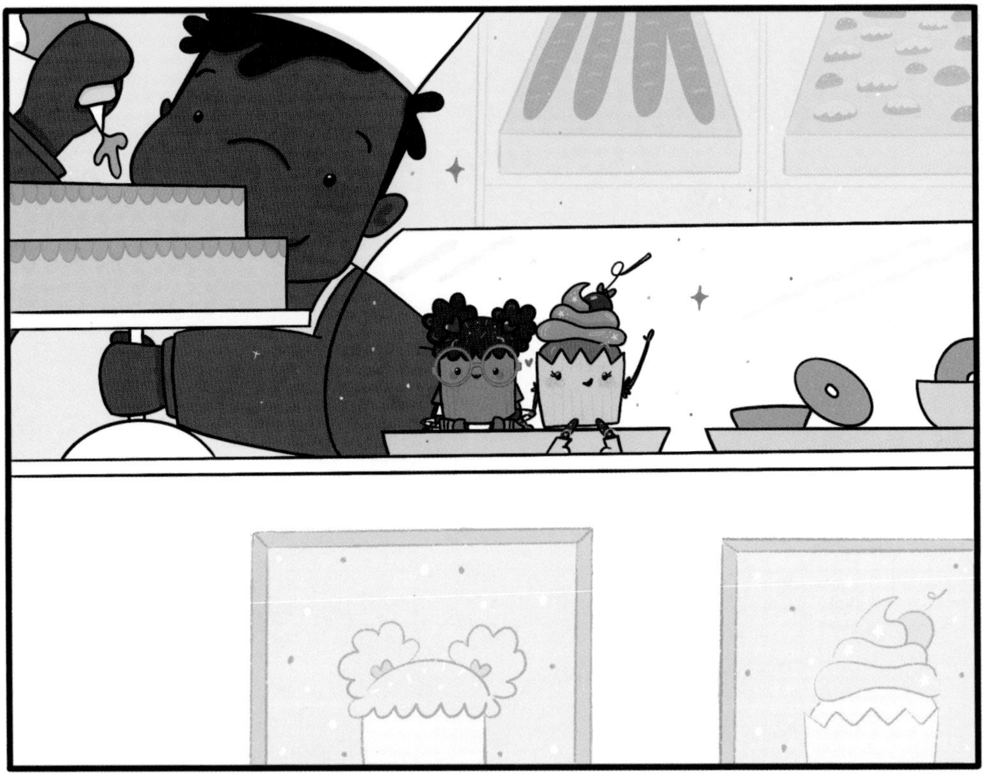

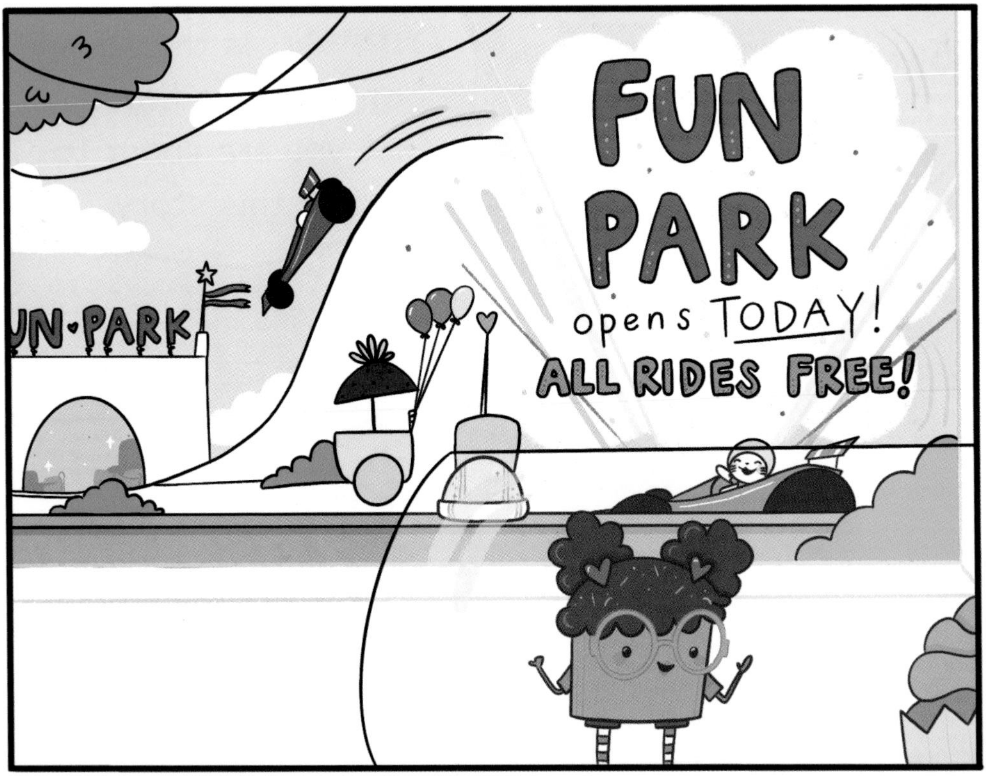
FUN PARK
opens TODAY!
ALL RIDES FREE!
UN·PARK

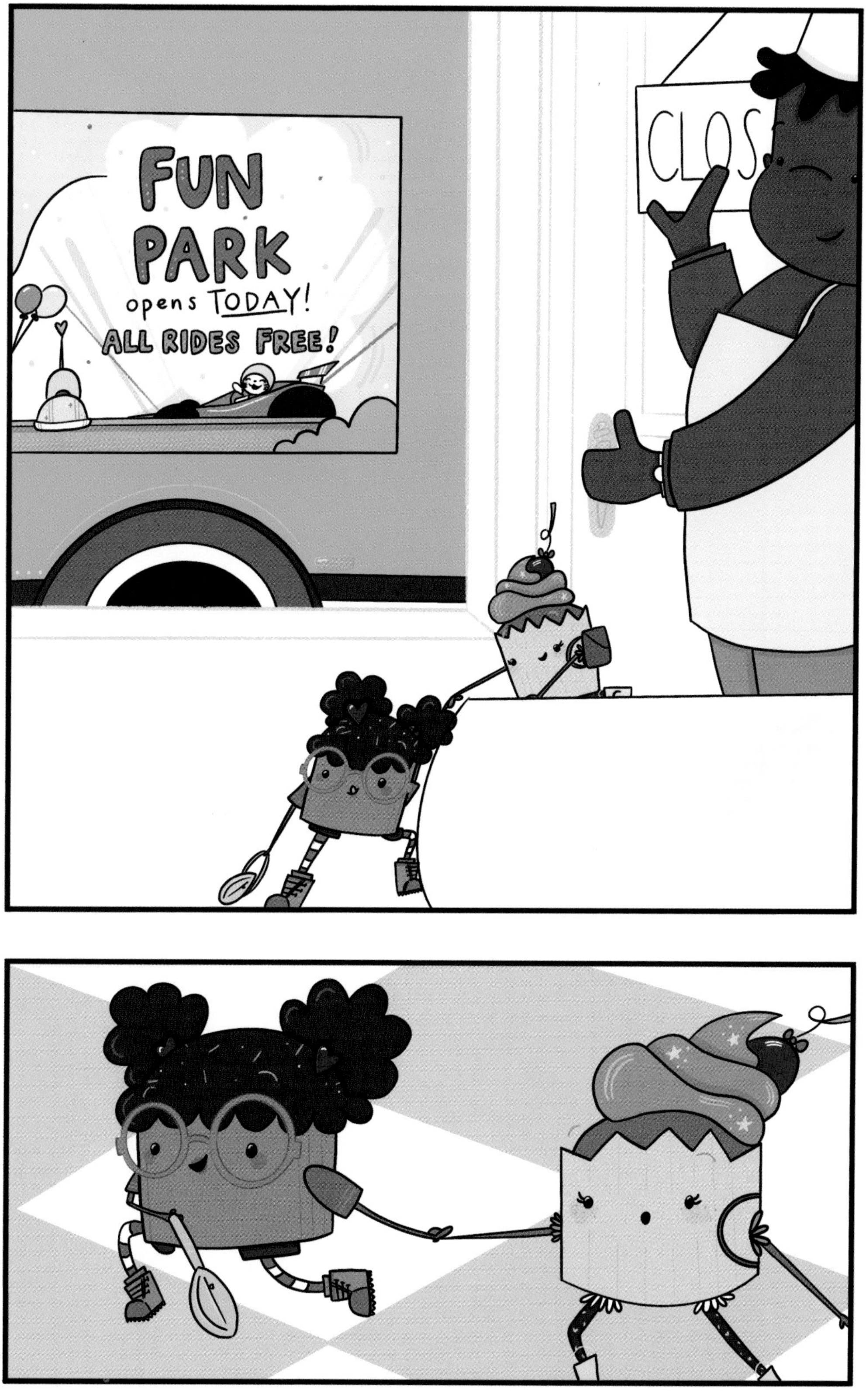
FUN PARK
opens TODAY!
ALL RIDES FREE!
CLOS

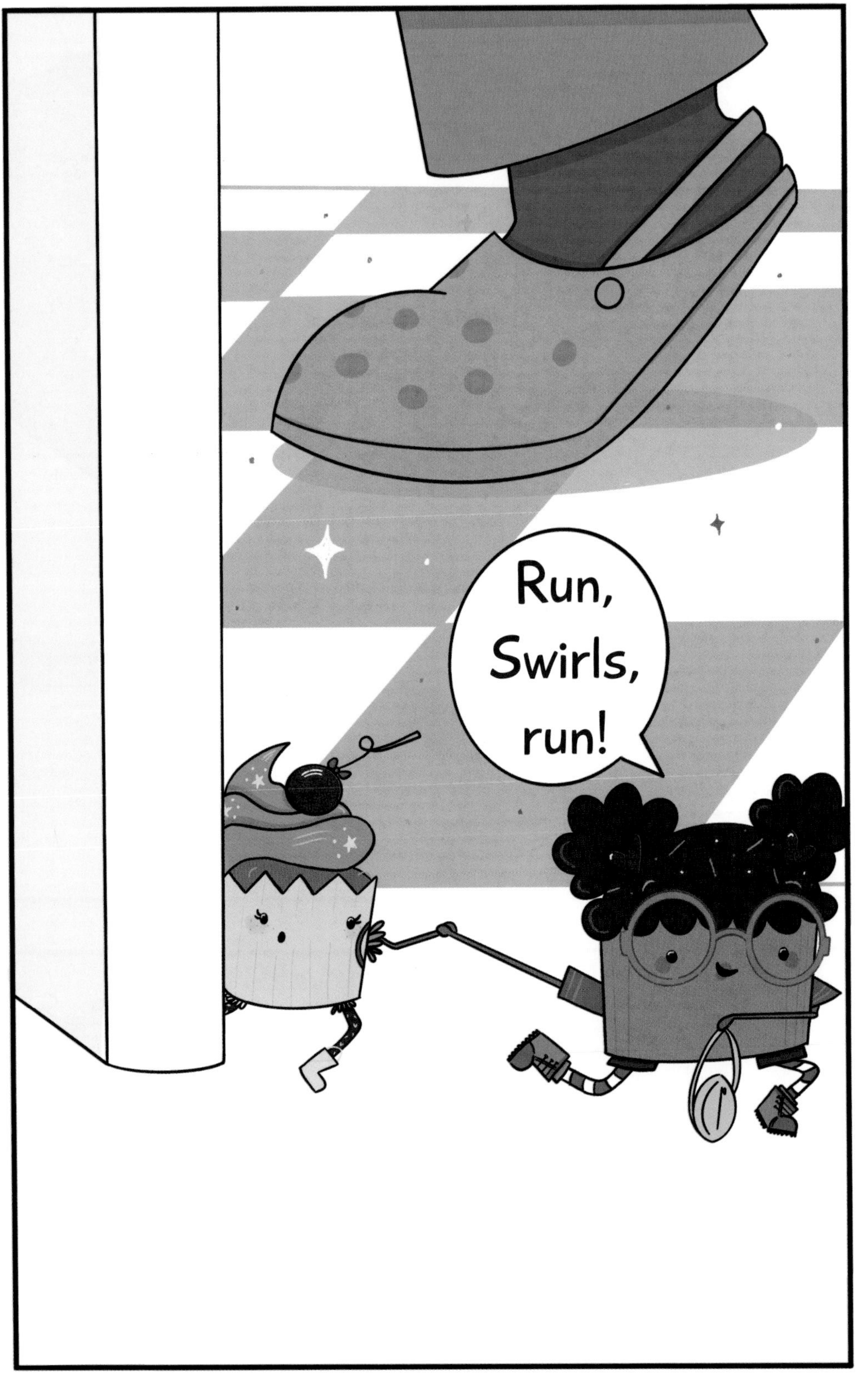
Run, Swirls, run!

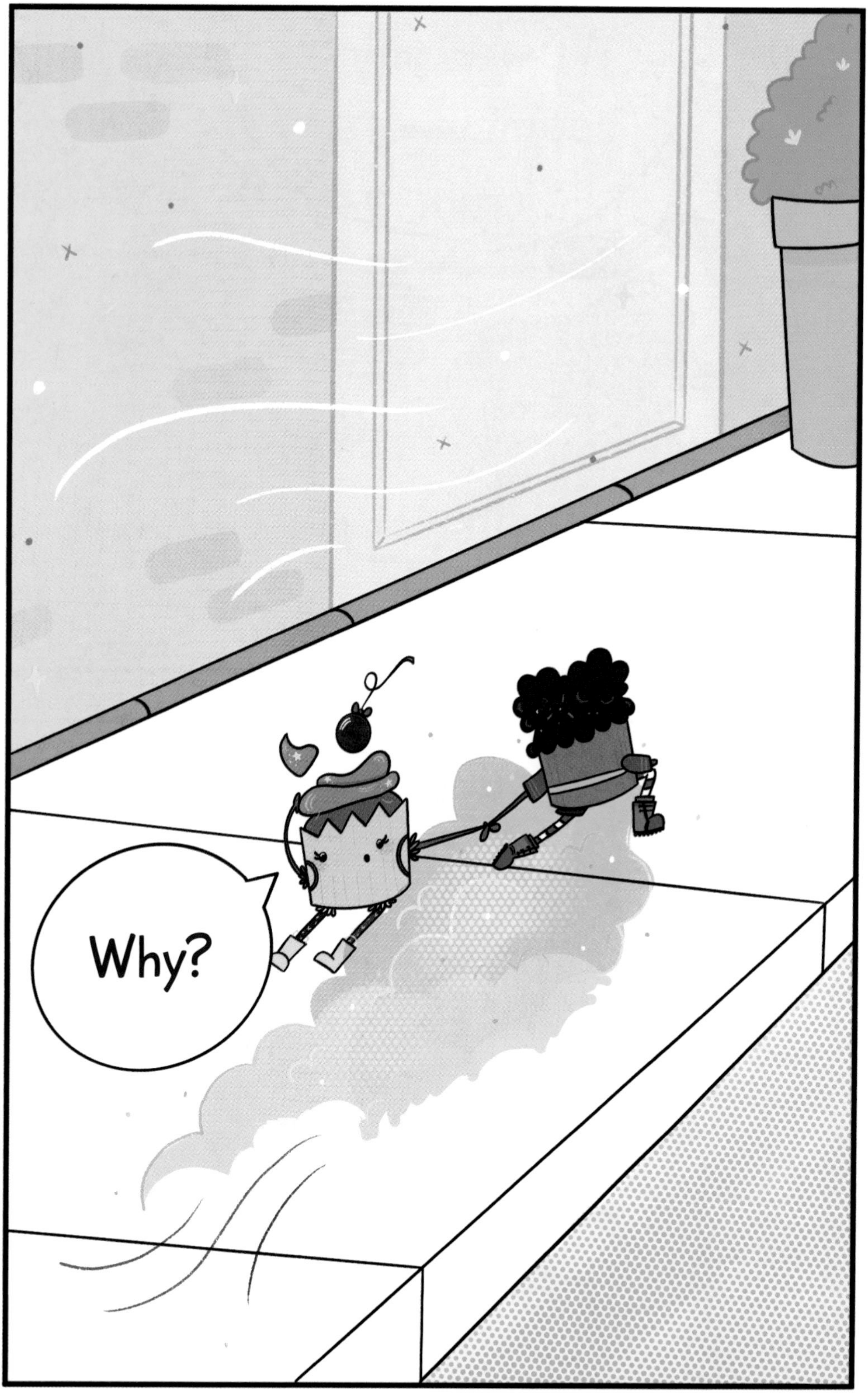
Why?

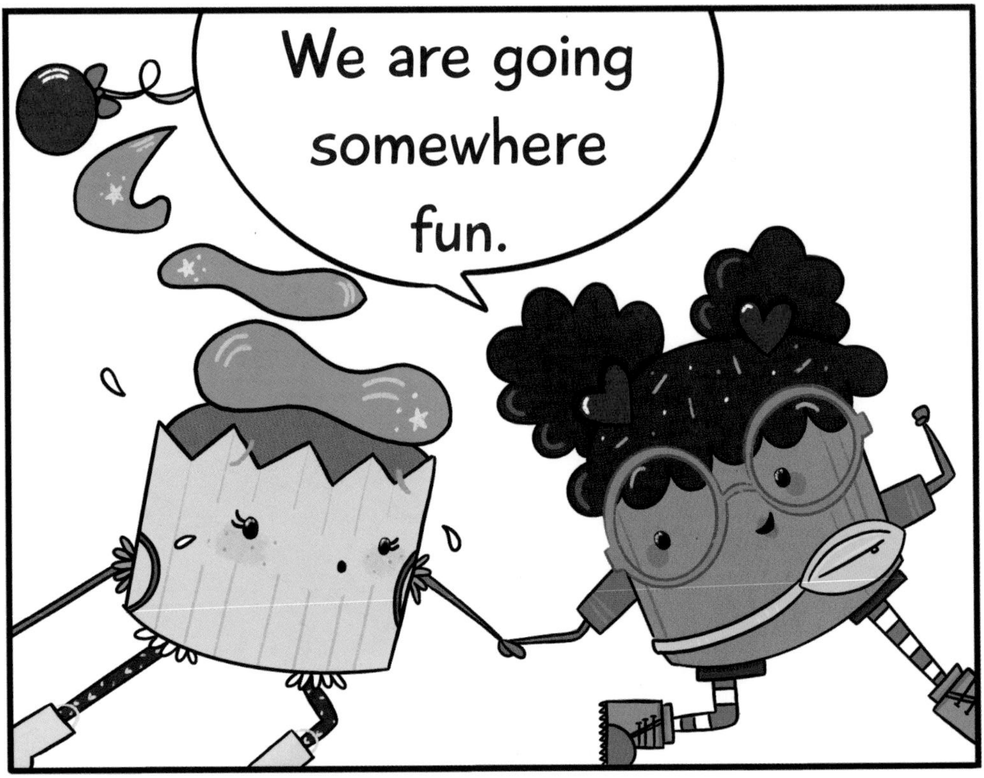
We are going somewhere fun.

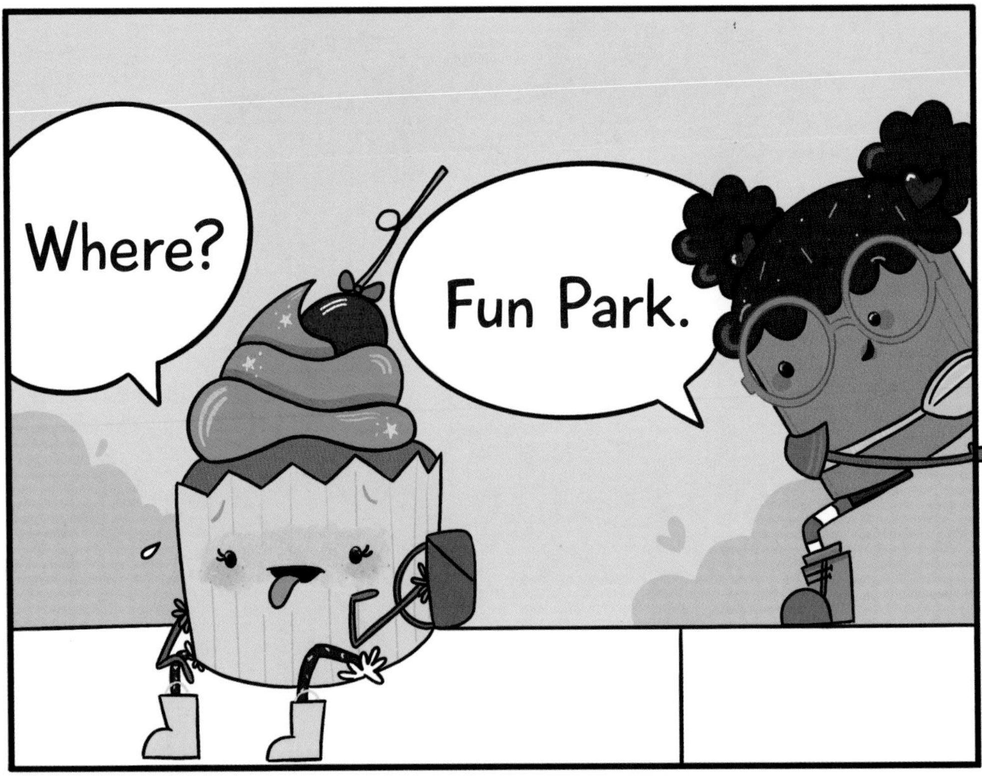
Where?
Fun Park.

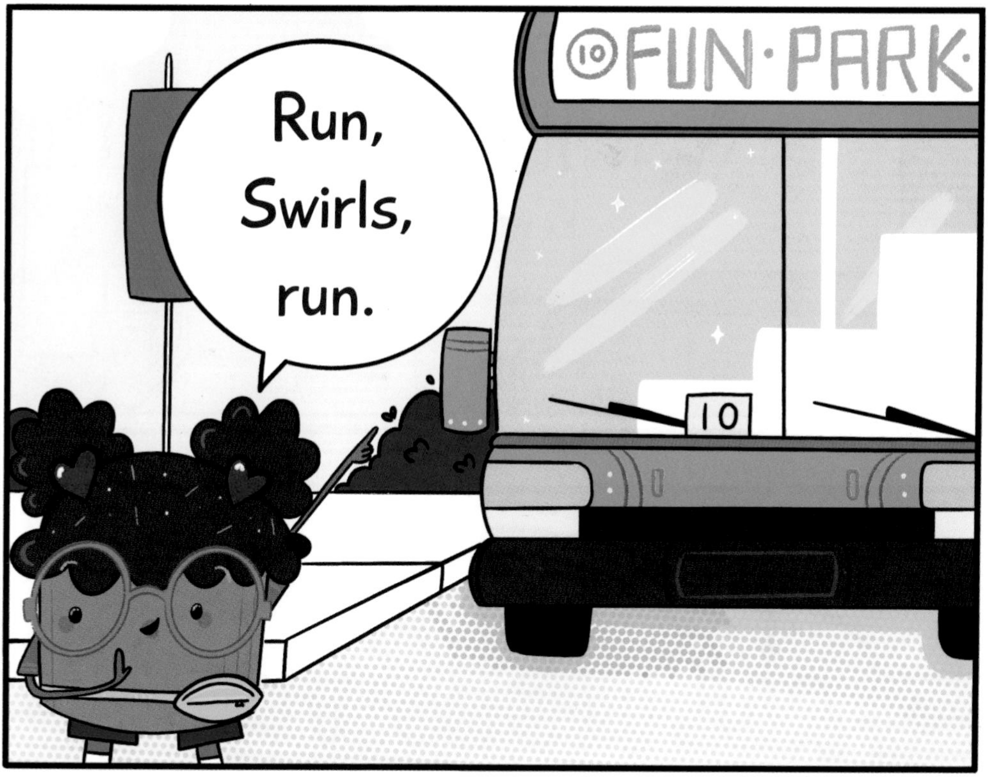
Run,
Swirls,
run.
FUN·PARK
10

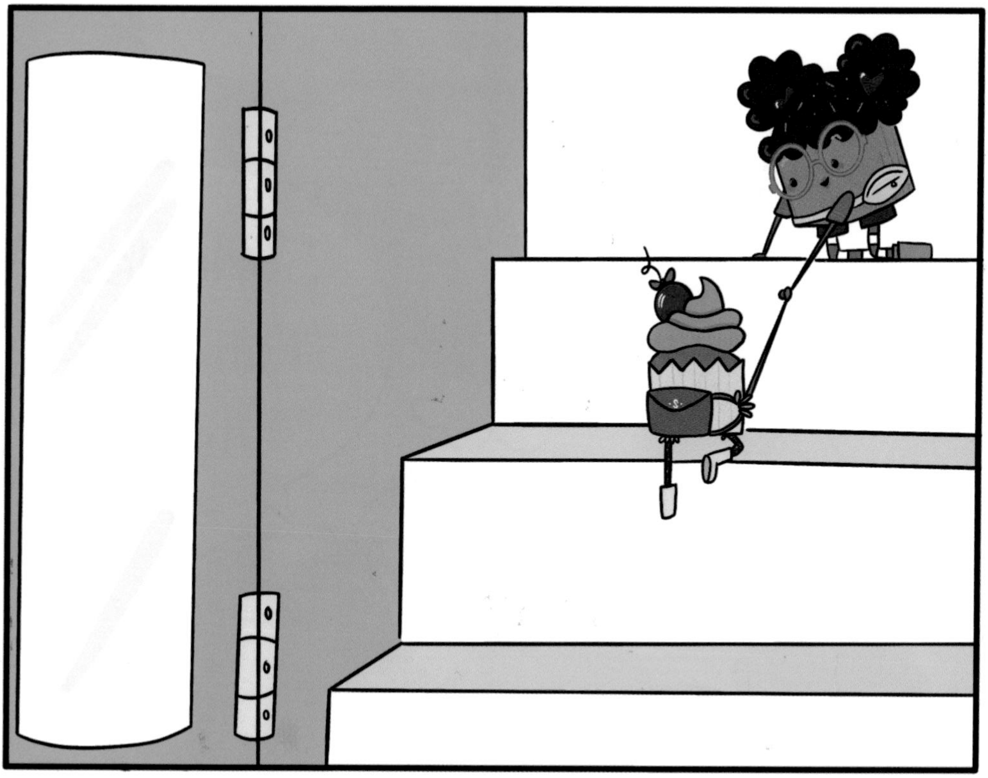

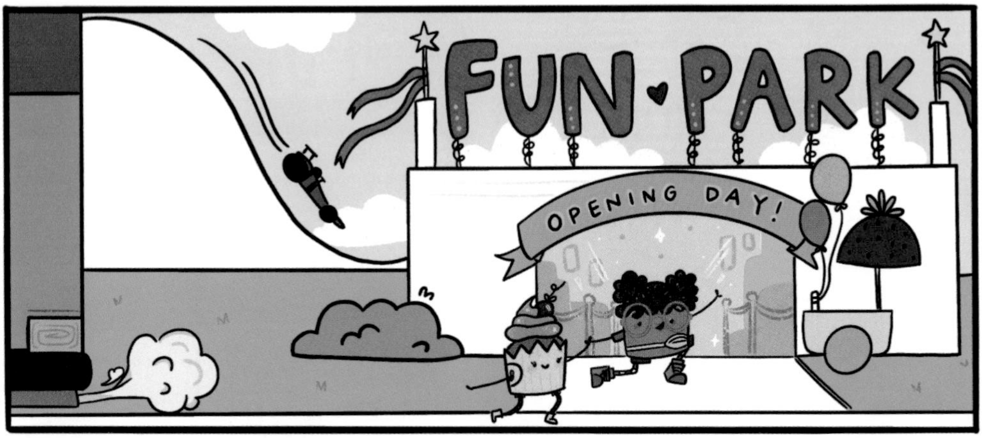
FUN PARK
OPENING DAY!

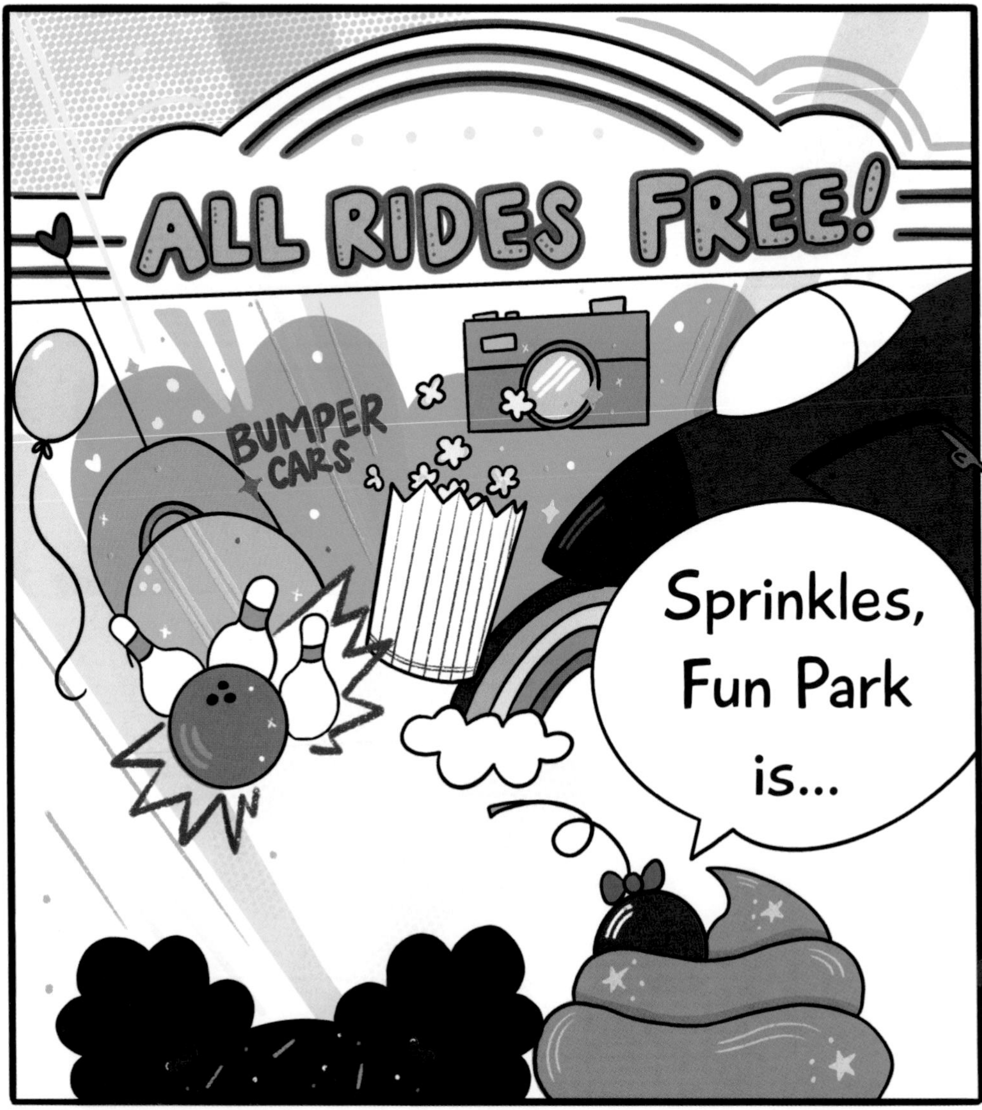
ALL RIDES FREE!
BUMPER CARS
Sprinkles, Fun Park is...

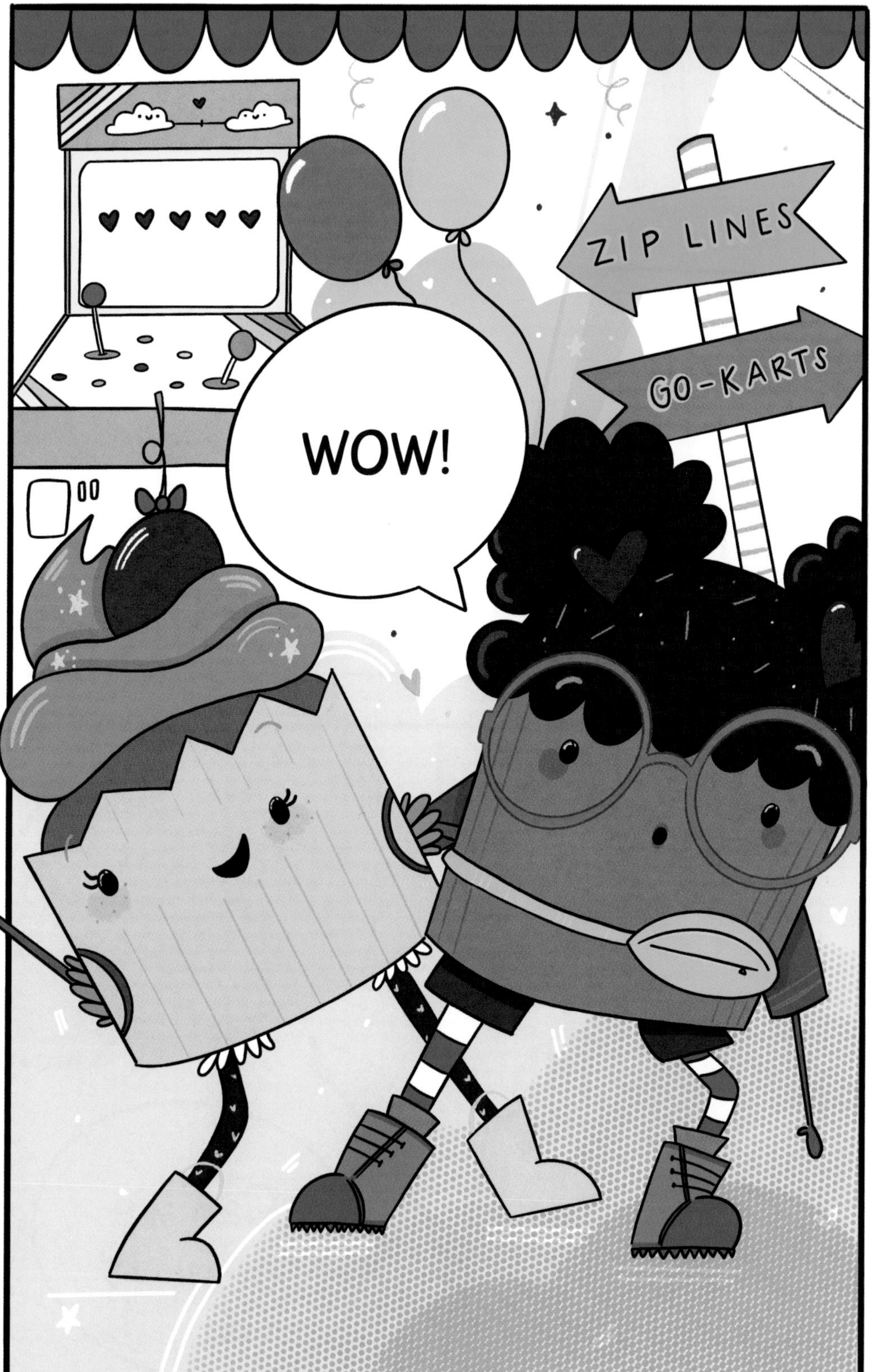
ZIP LINES
GO-KARTS
WOW!

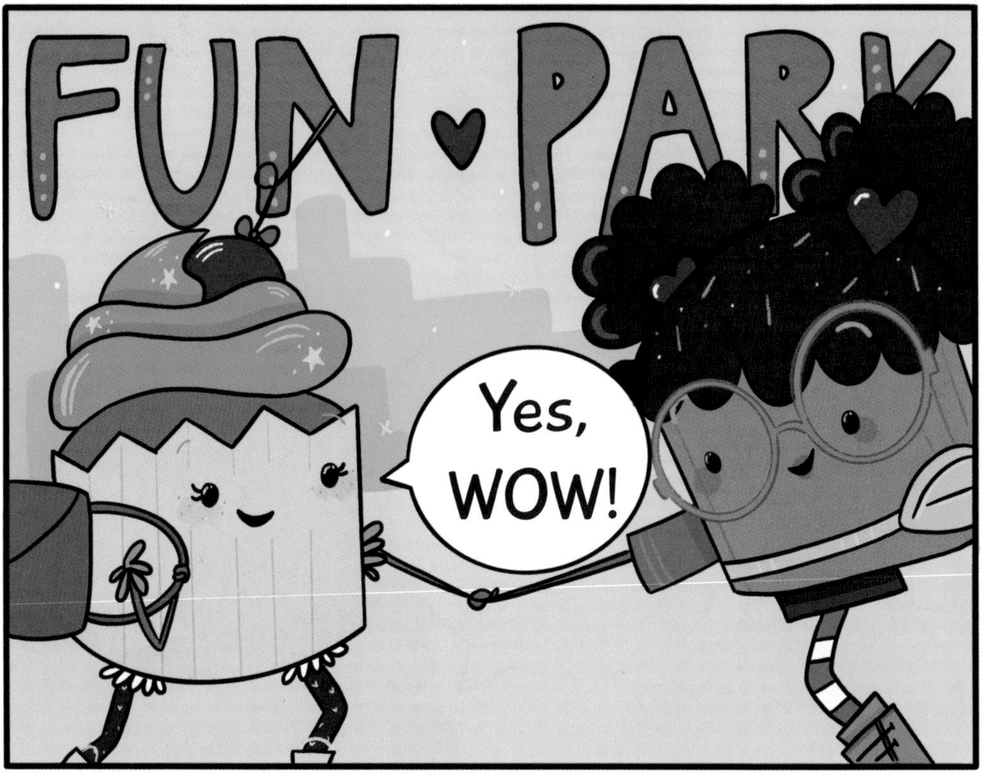
FUN PARK
Yes, WOW!

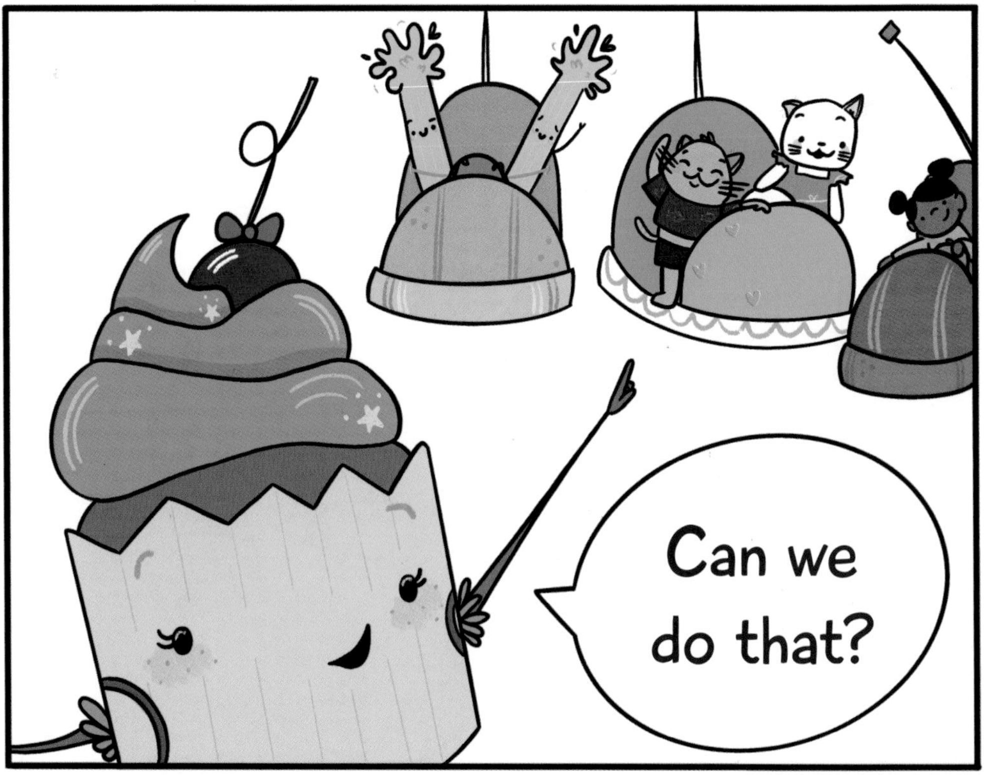
Can we do that?

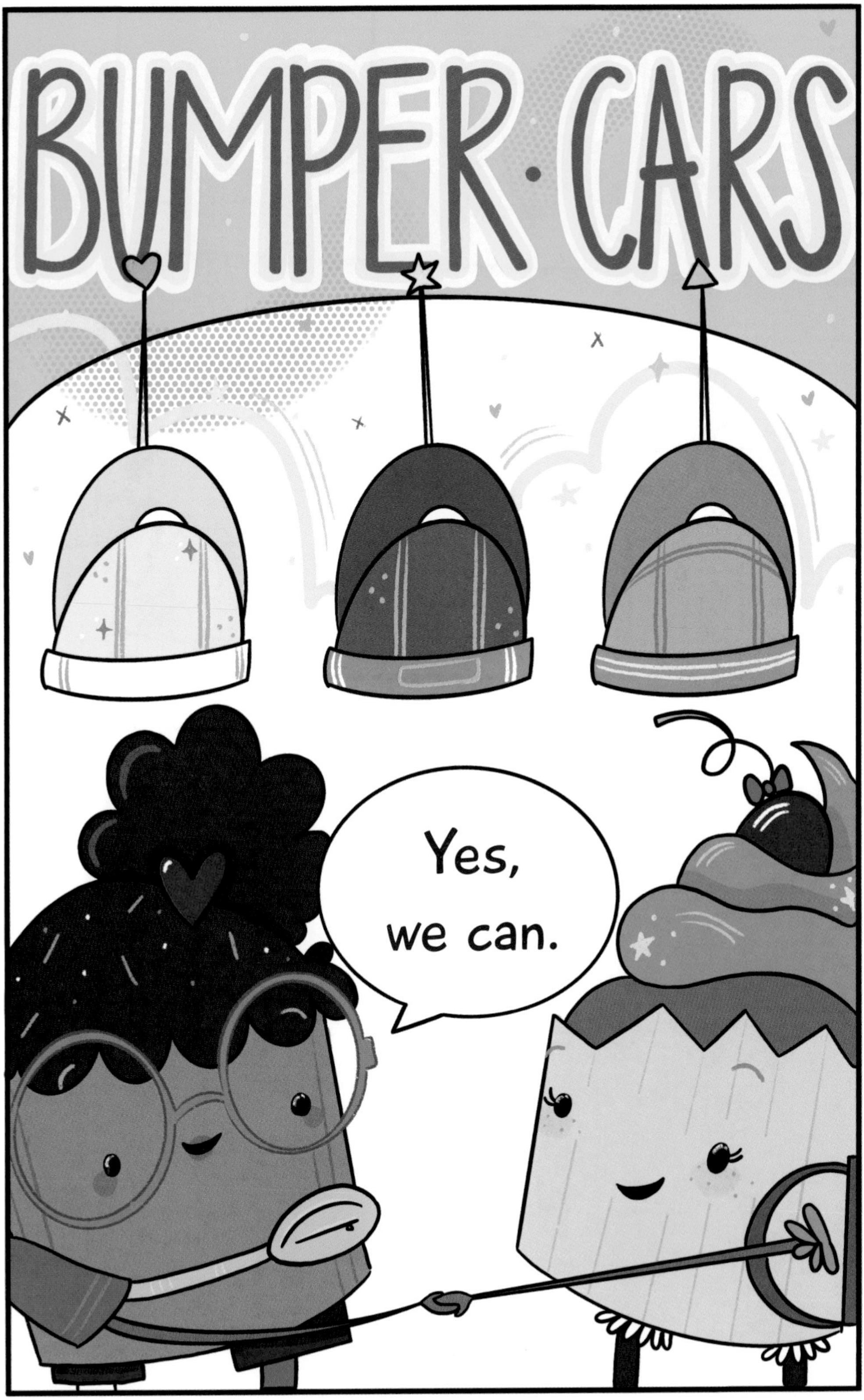
BUMPER CARS
Yes, we can.

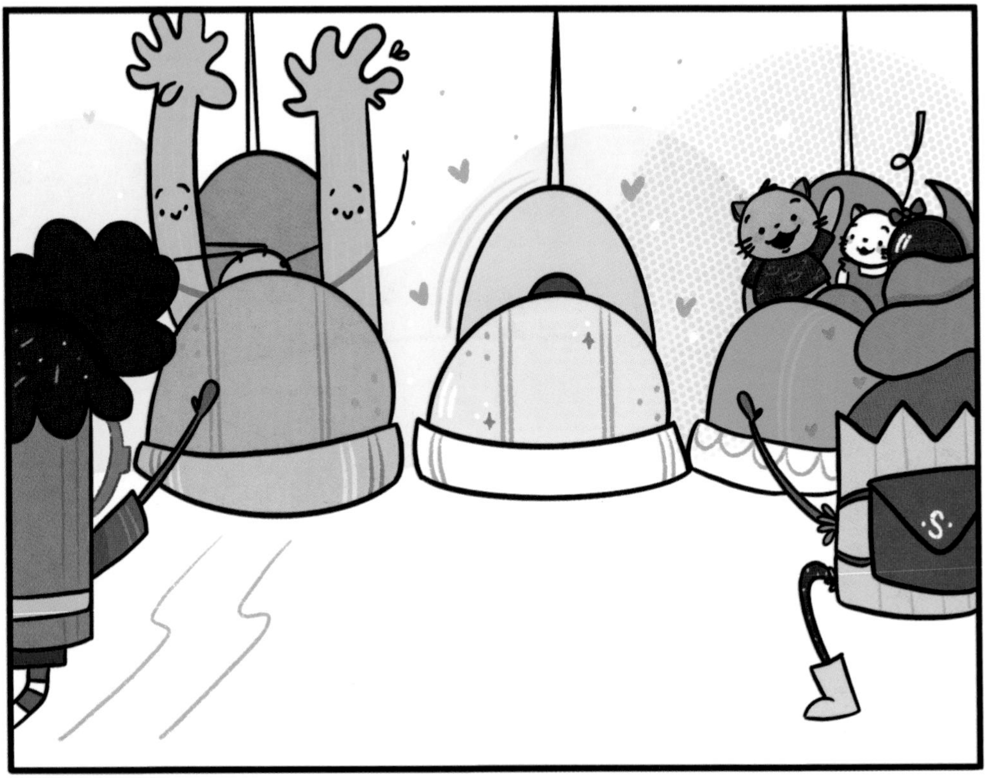

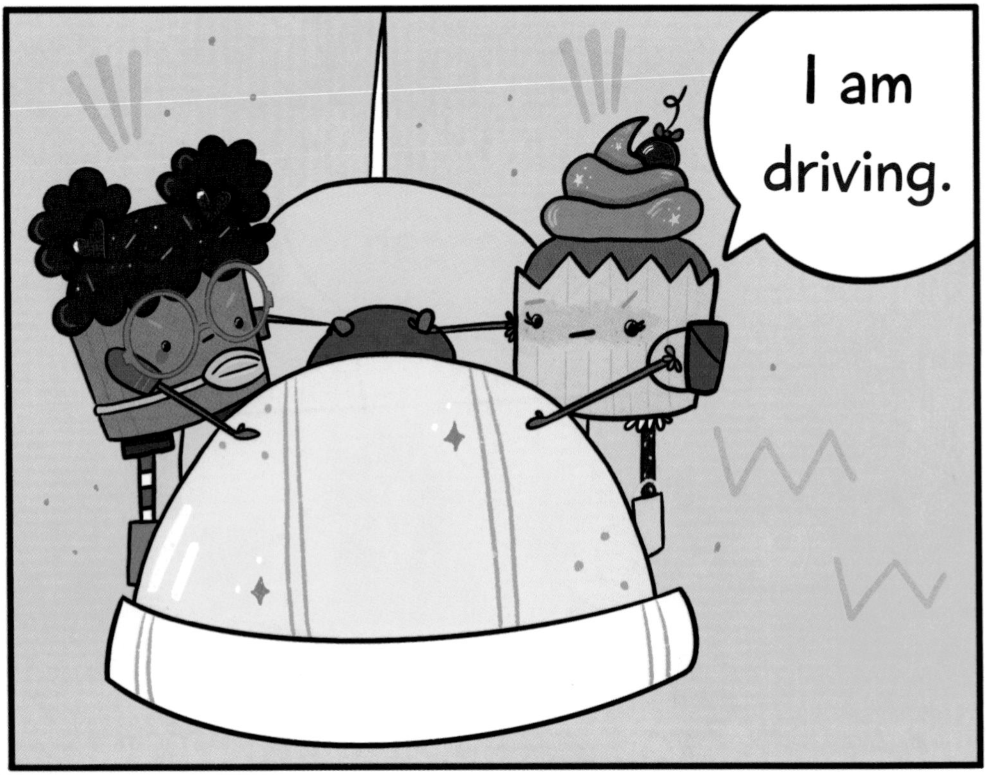
I am driving.

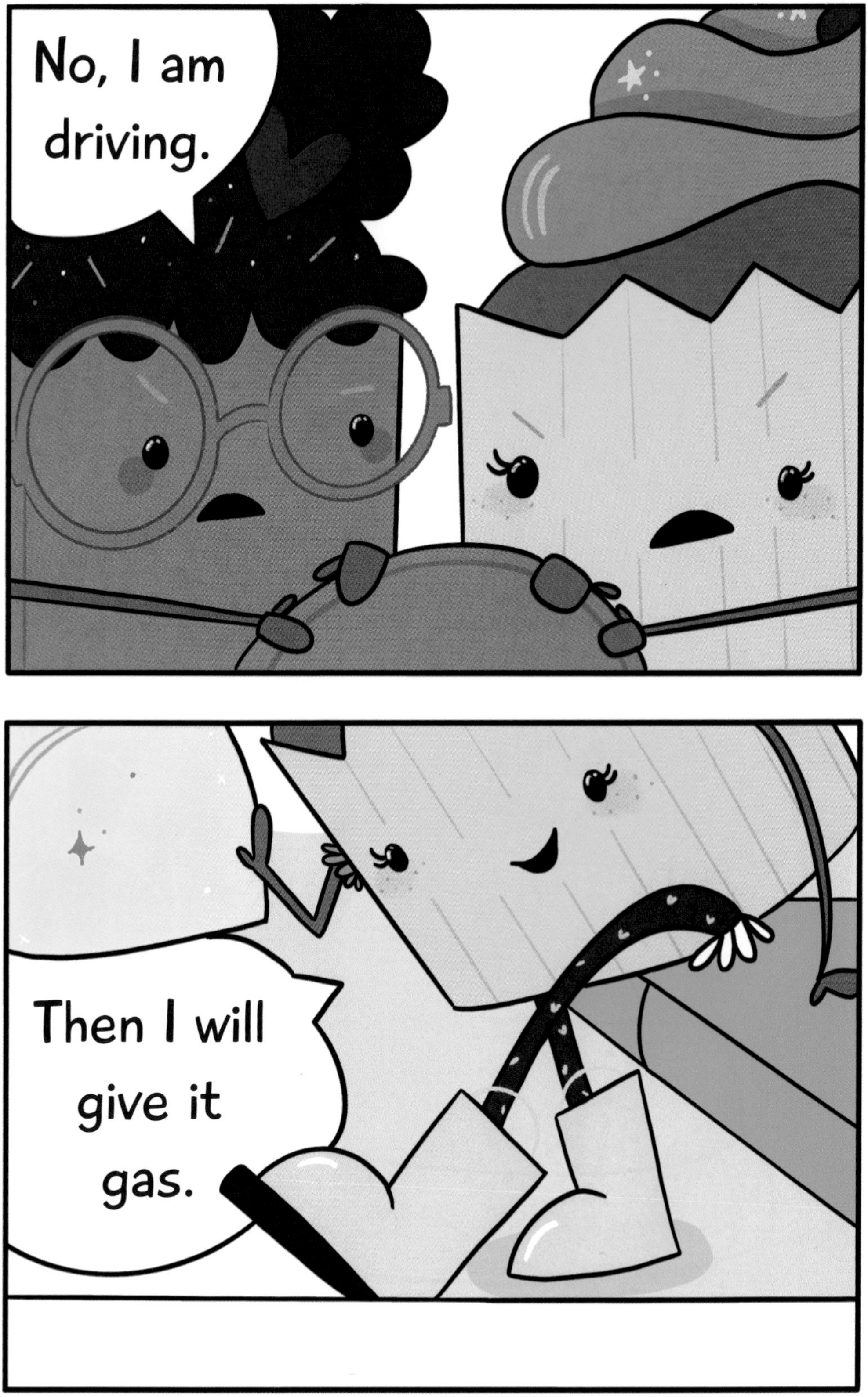
No, I am driving.
Then I will give it gas.

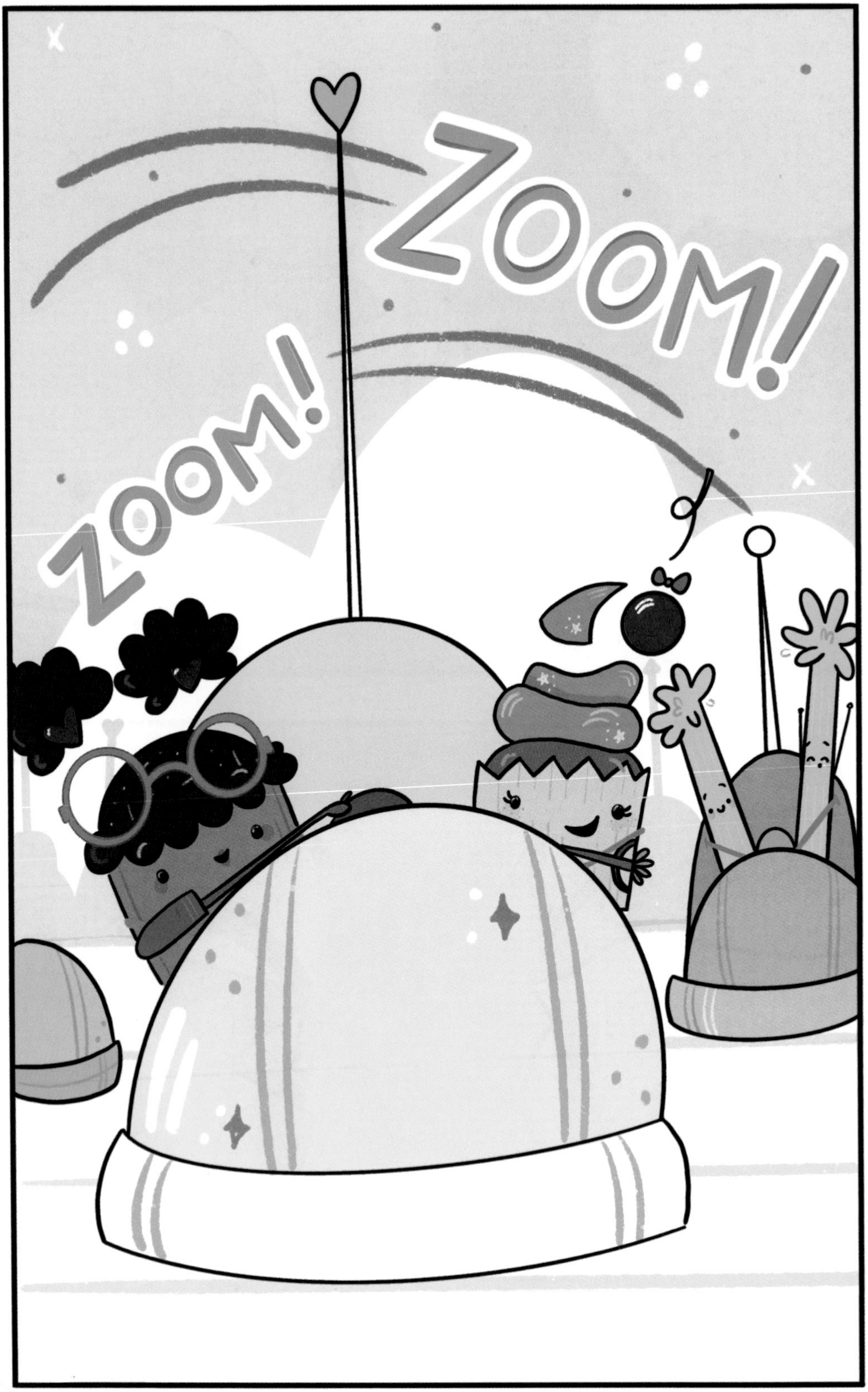
ZOOM!
ZOOM!

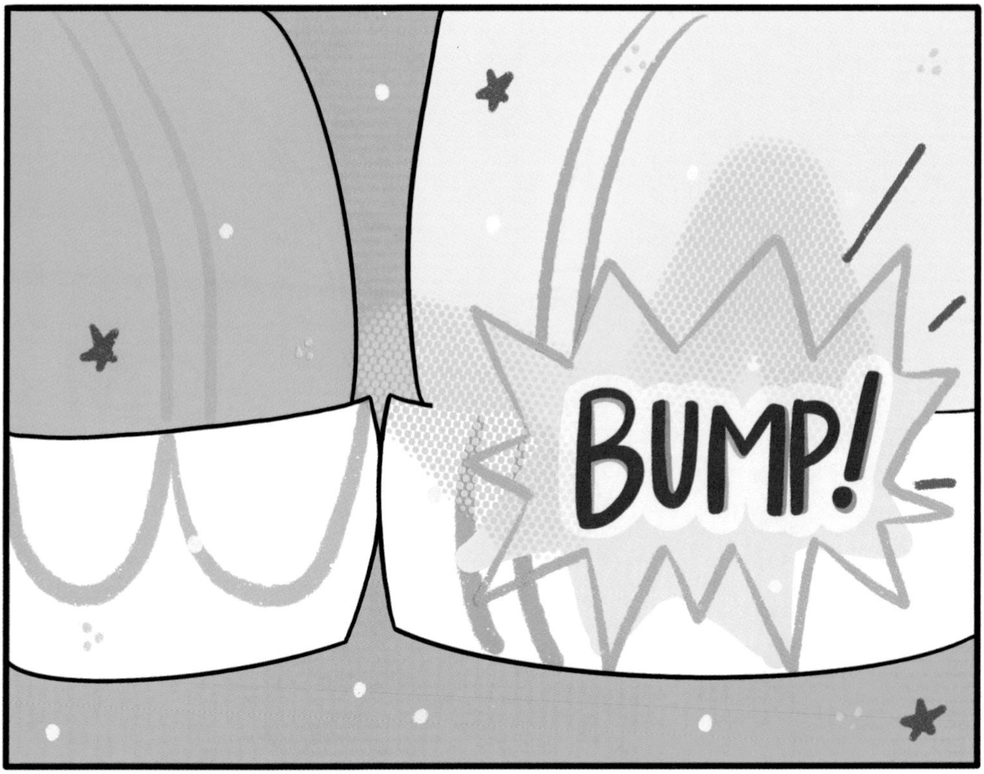
BUMP!

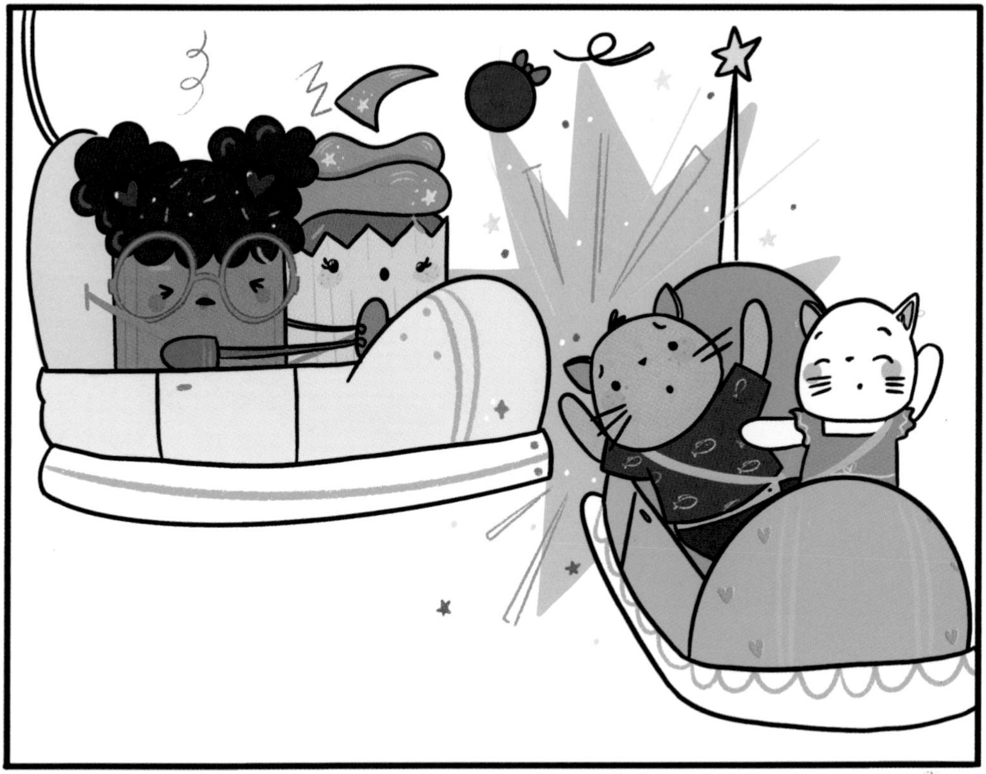

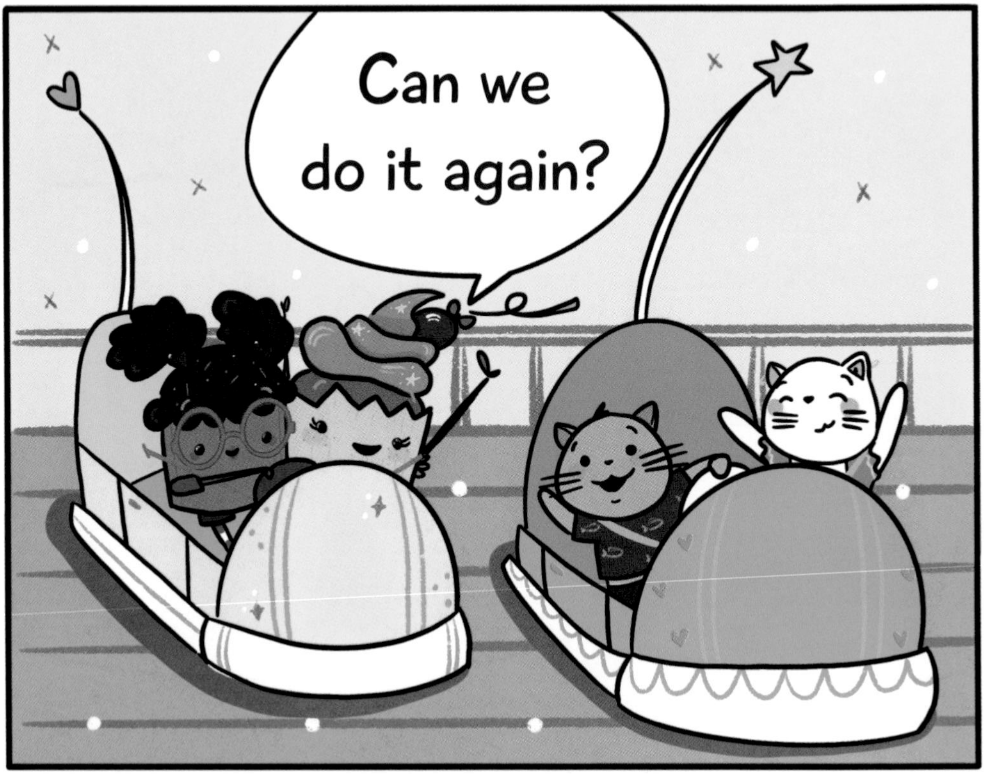
Can we do it again?

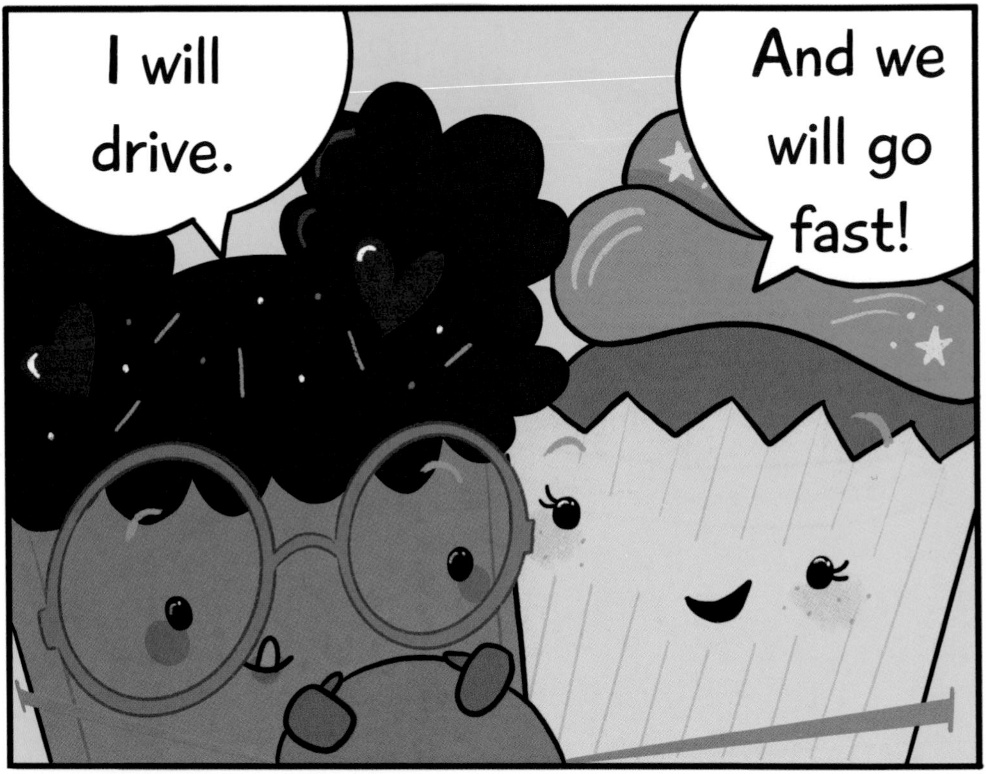
I will drive.
And we will go fast!

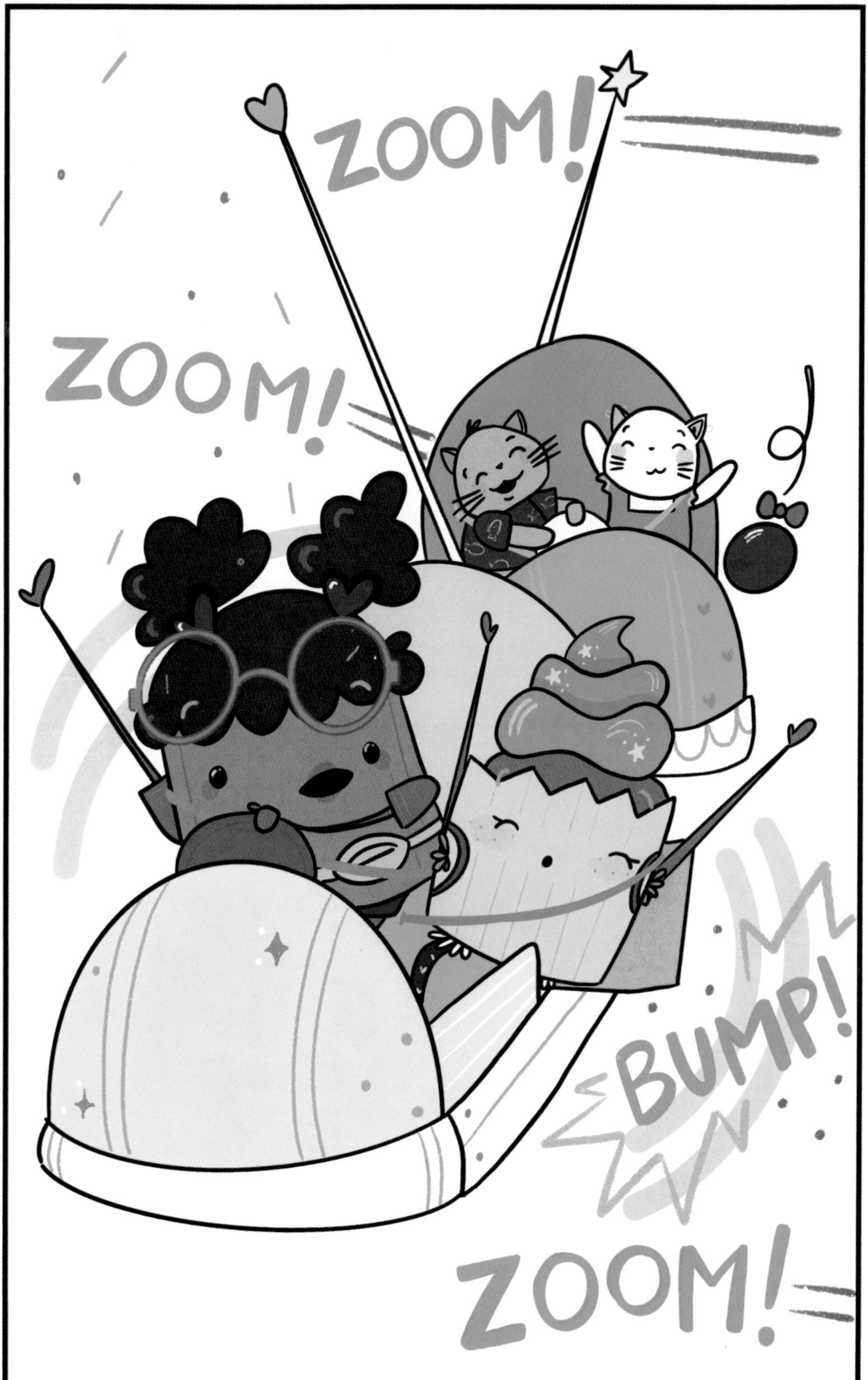
ZOOM!
ZOOM!
BUMP!
ZOOM!

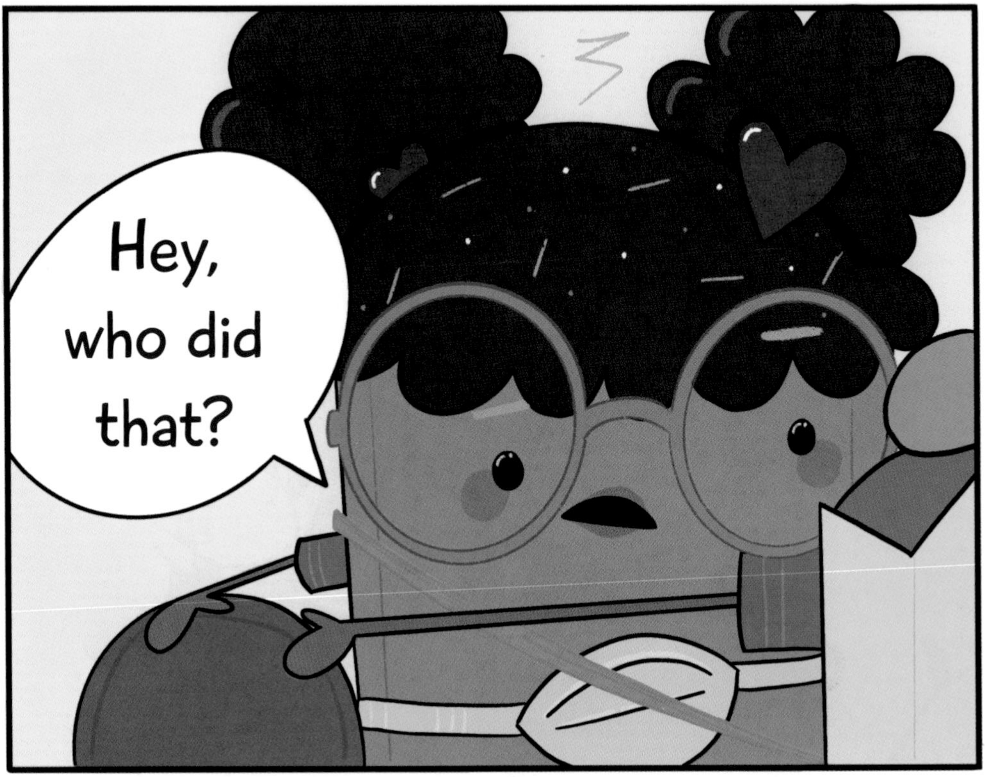
Hey, who did that?

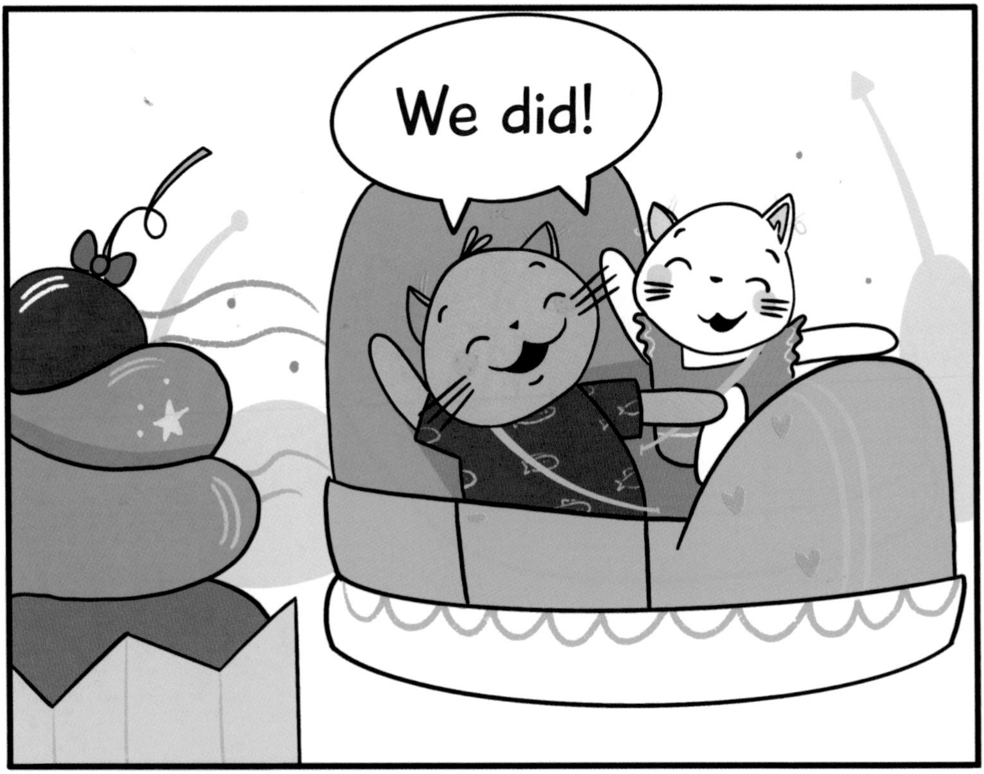
We did!

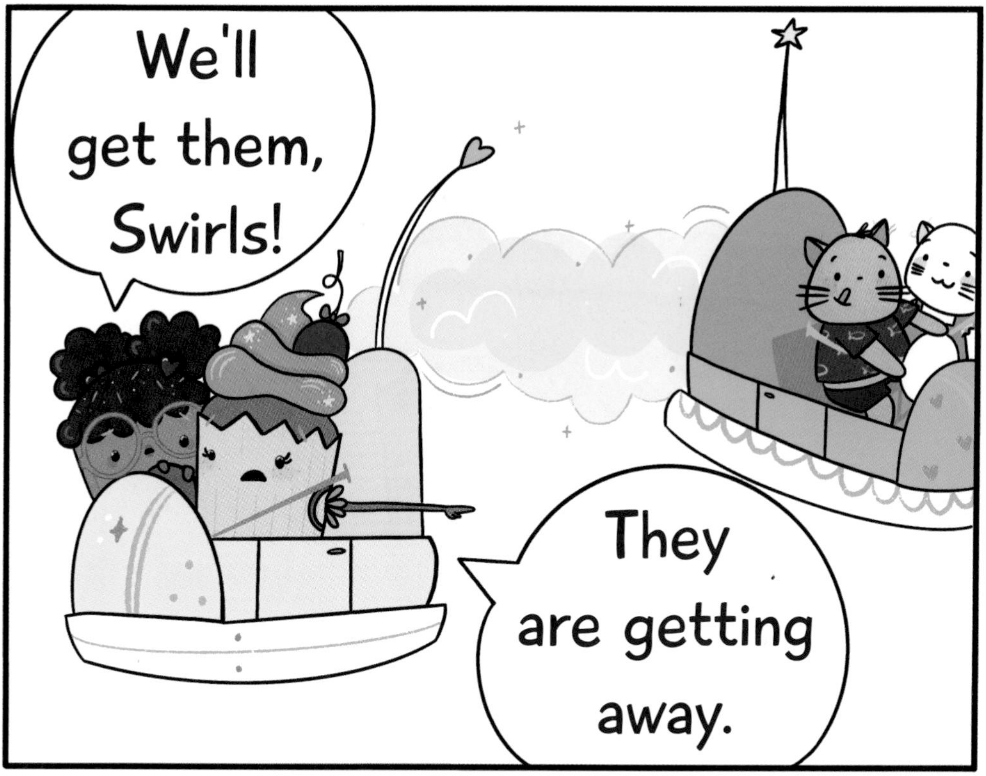
We'll get them, Swirls!
They are getting away.

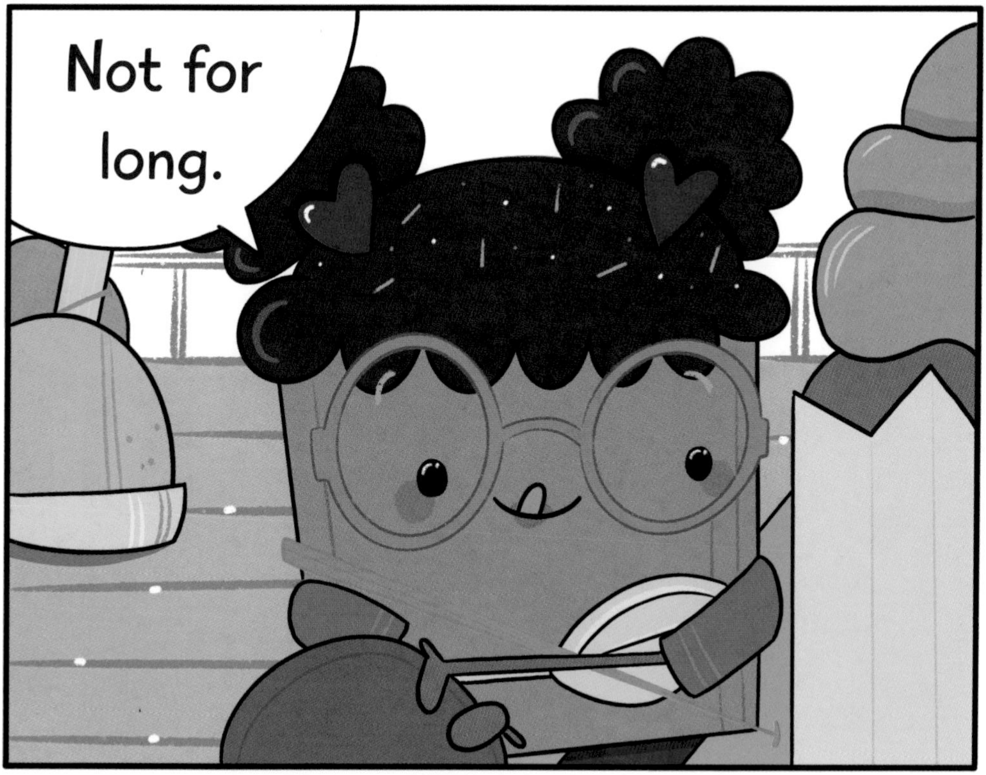
Not for long.

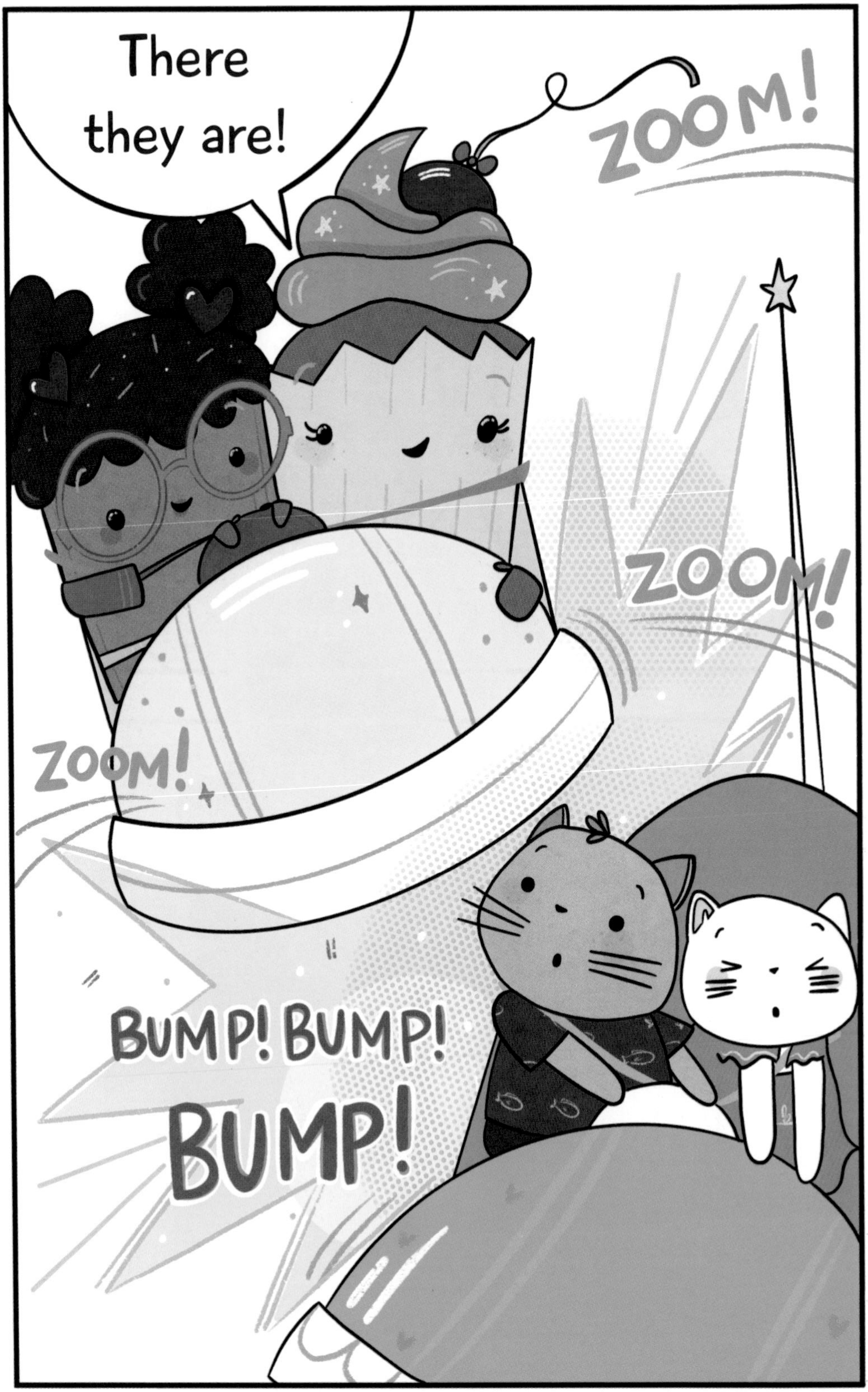
There they are!
ZOOM!
ZOOM!
ZOOM!
BUMP! BUMP!
BUMP!

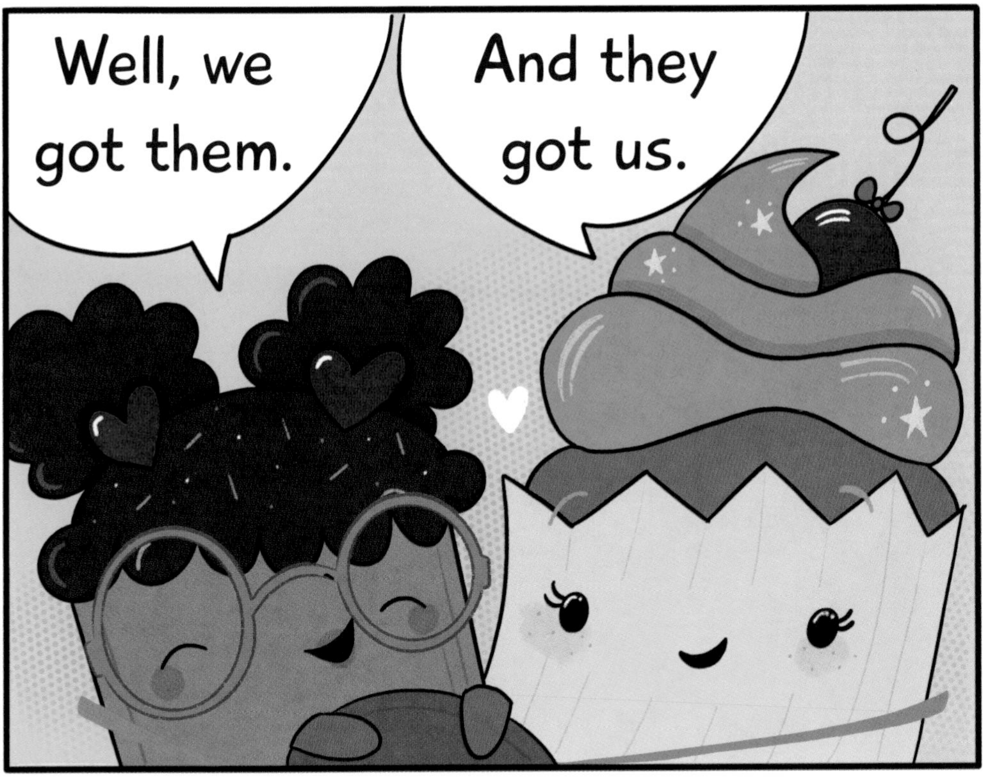
Well, we got them.
And they got us.

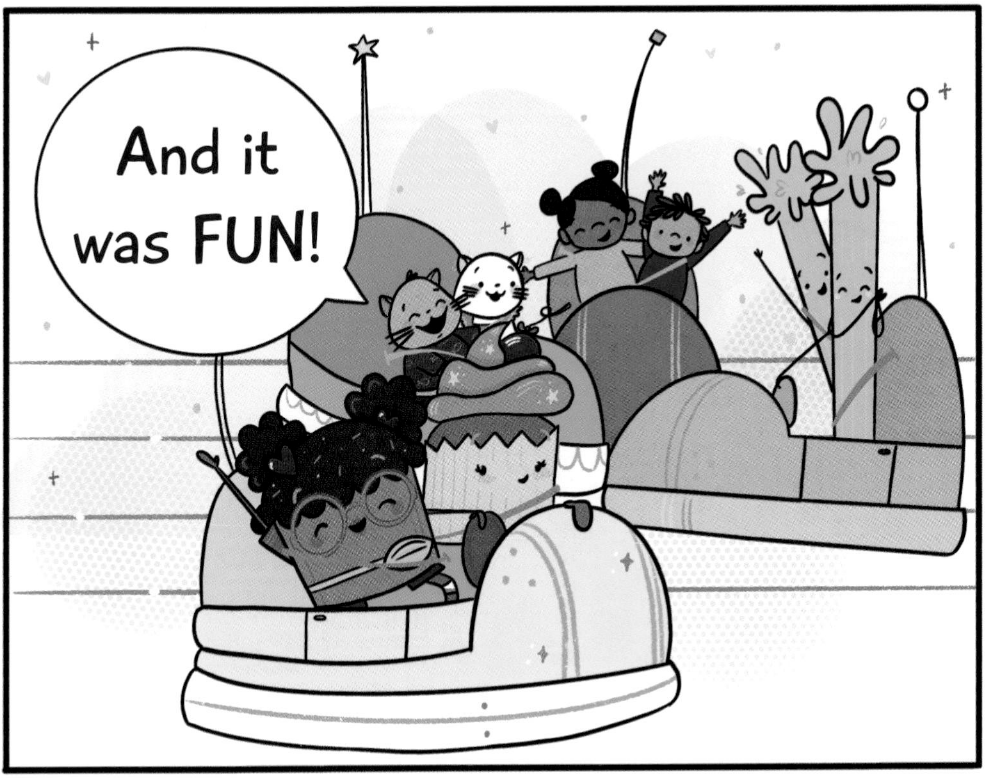
And it was FUN!

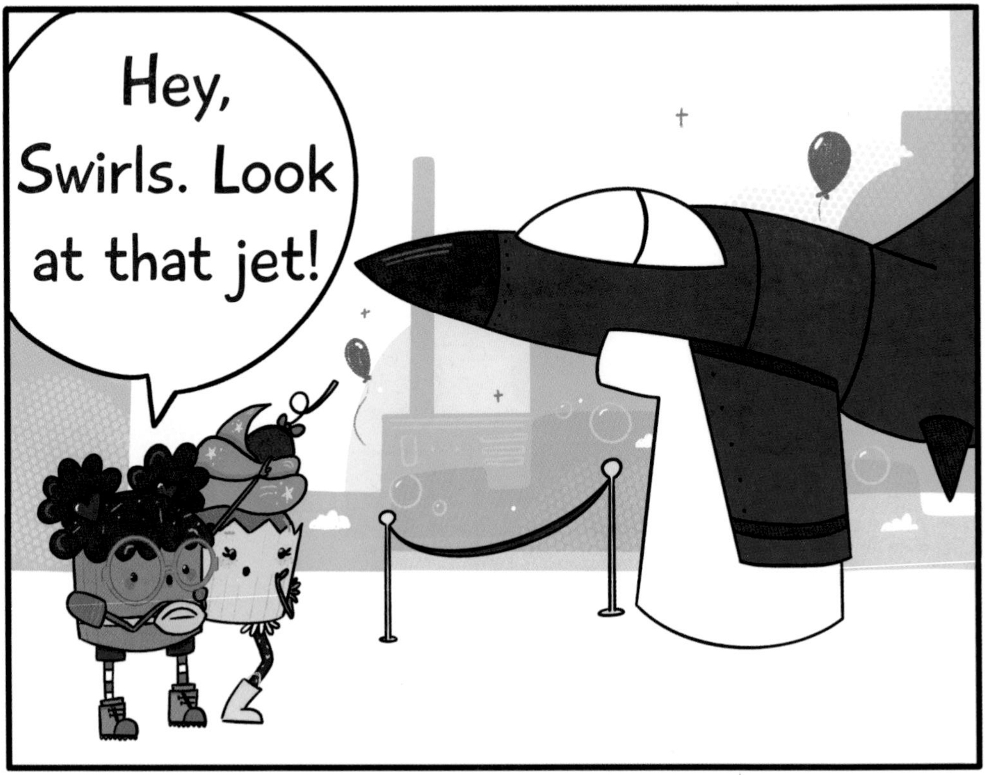
Hey, Swirls. Look at that jet!

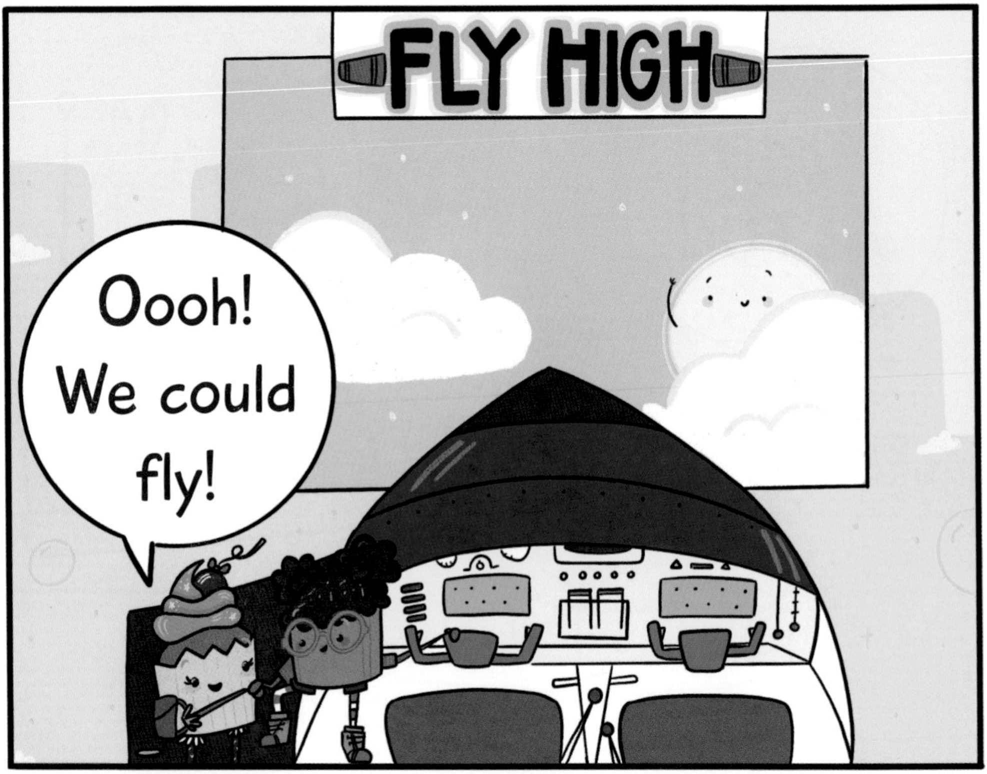
FLY HIGH
Oooh! We could fly!

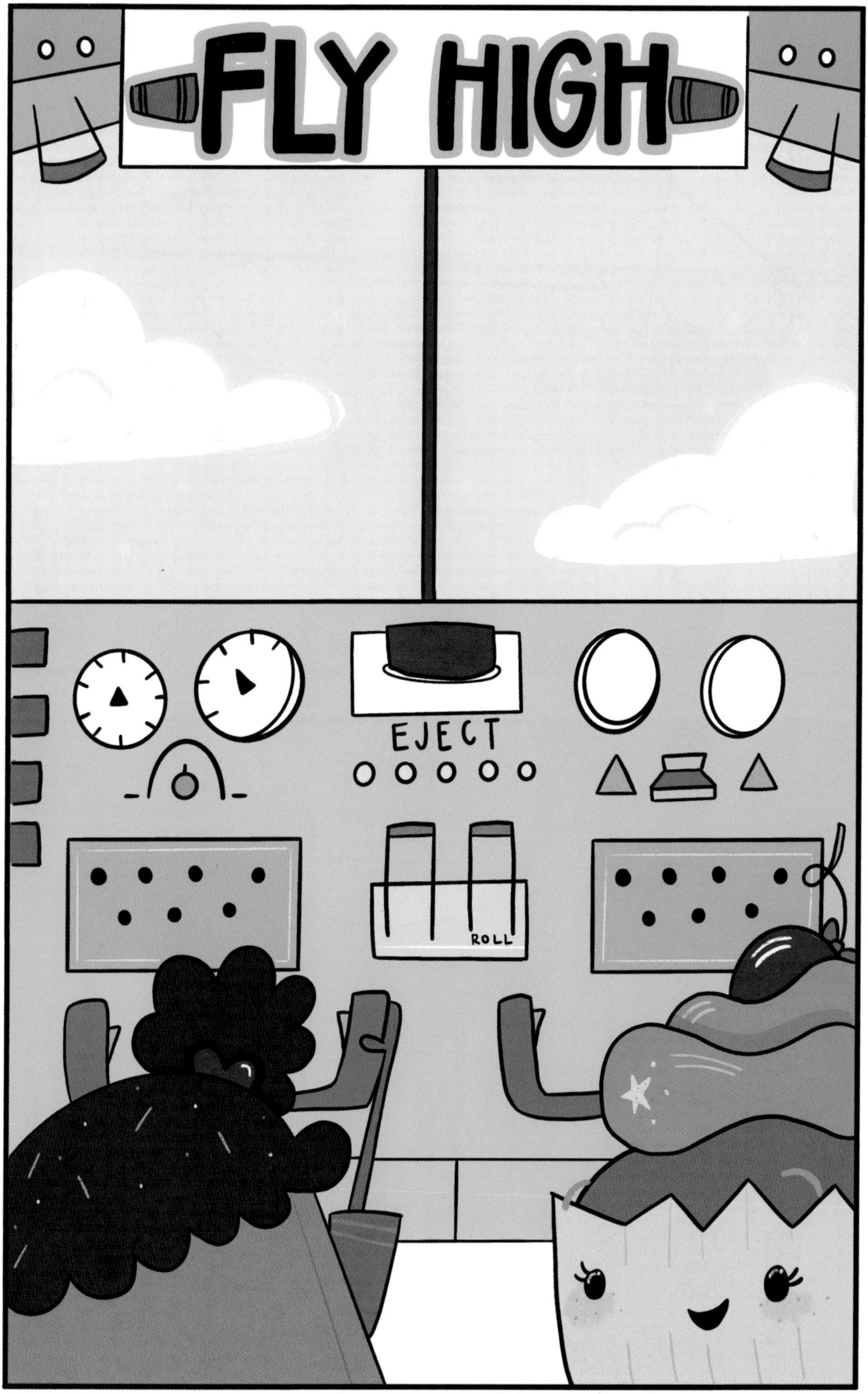
FLY HIGH
EJECT
ROLL

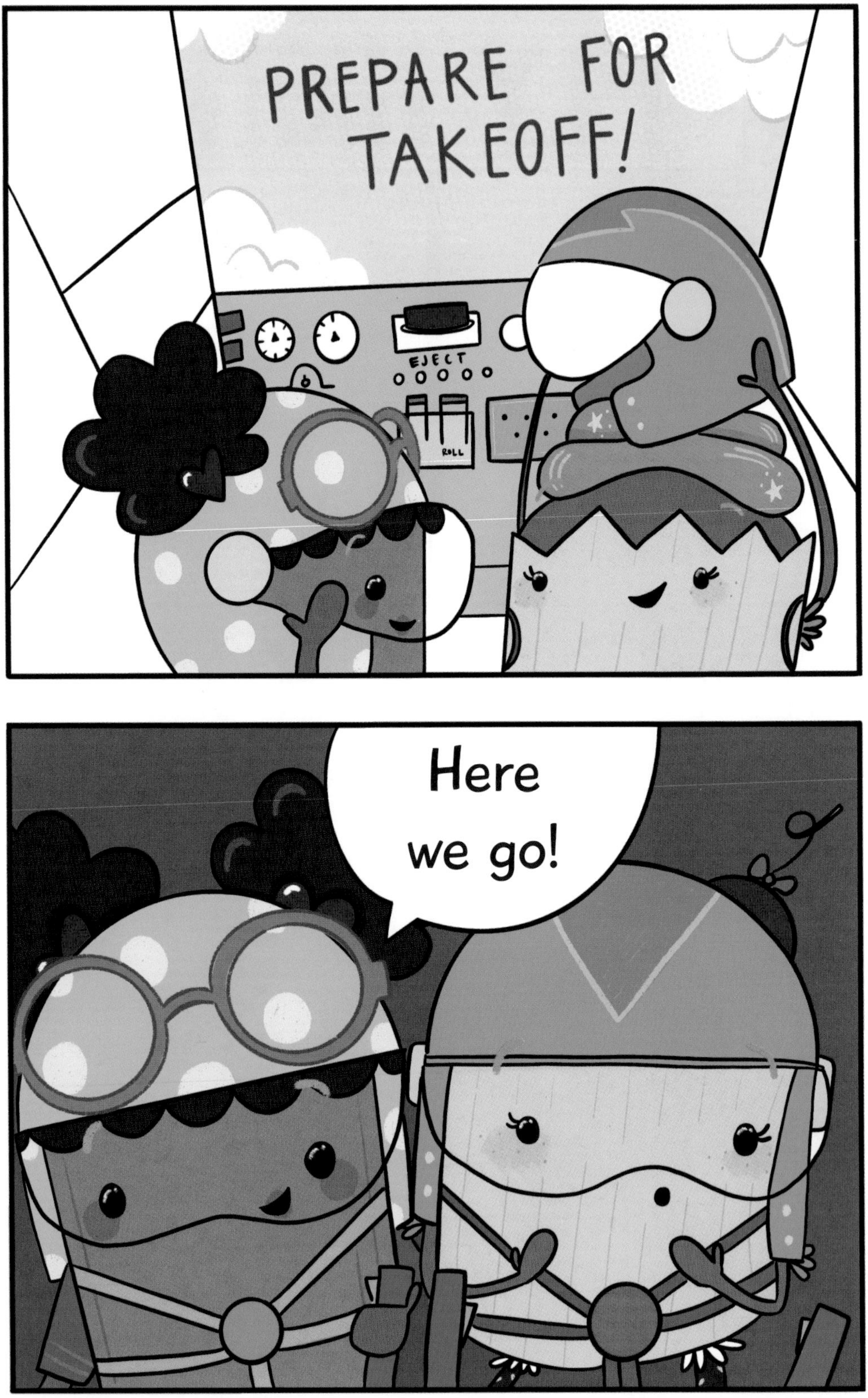
PREPARE FOR TAKEOFF!
EJECT
ROLL
Here we go!

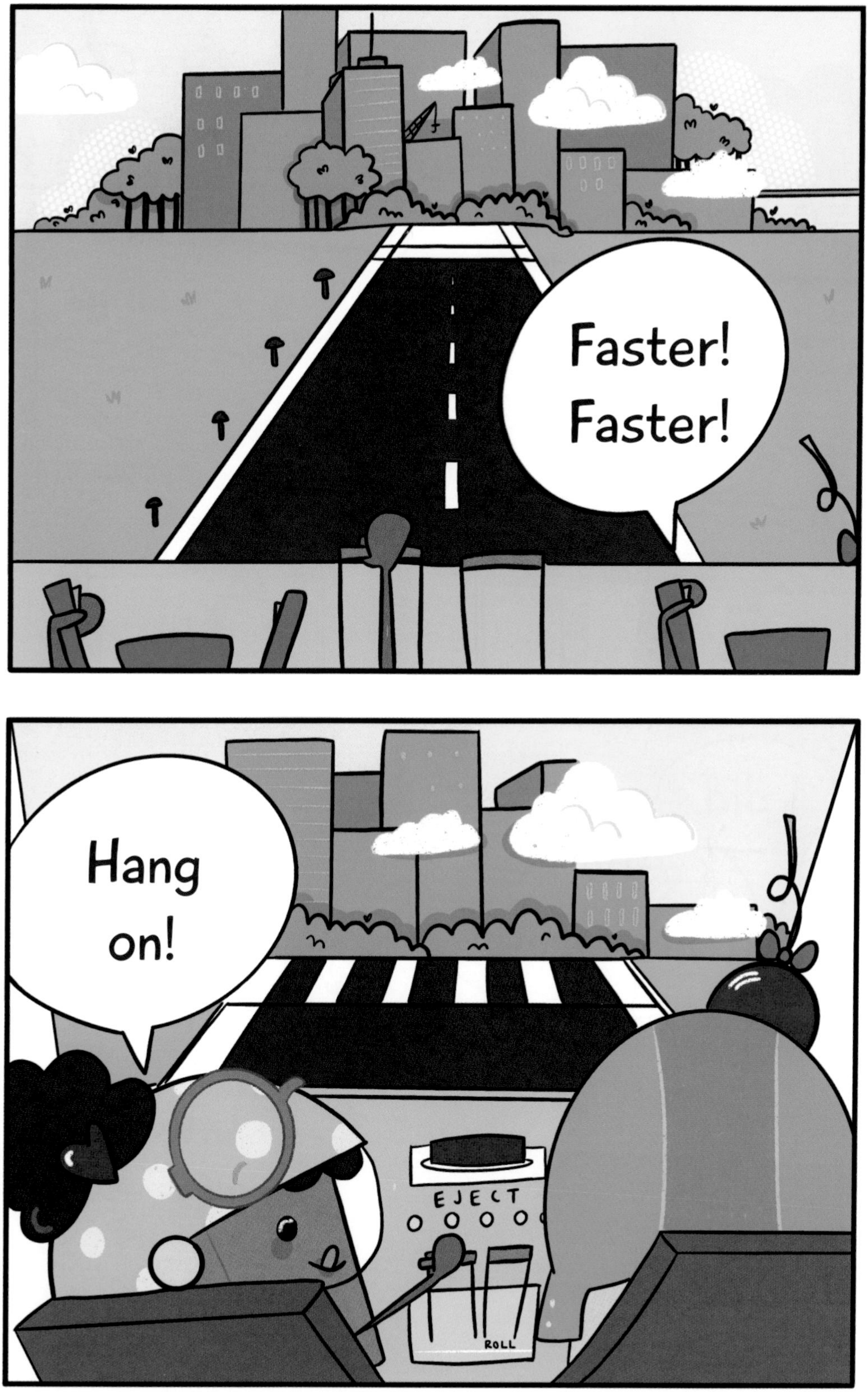
Faster! Faster!
Hang on!
EJECT
ROLL

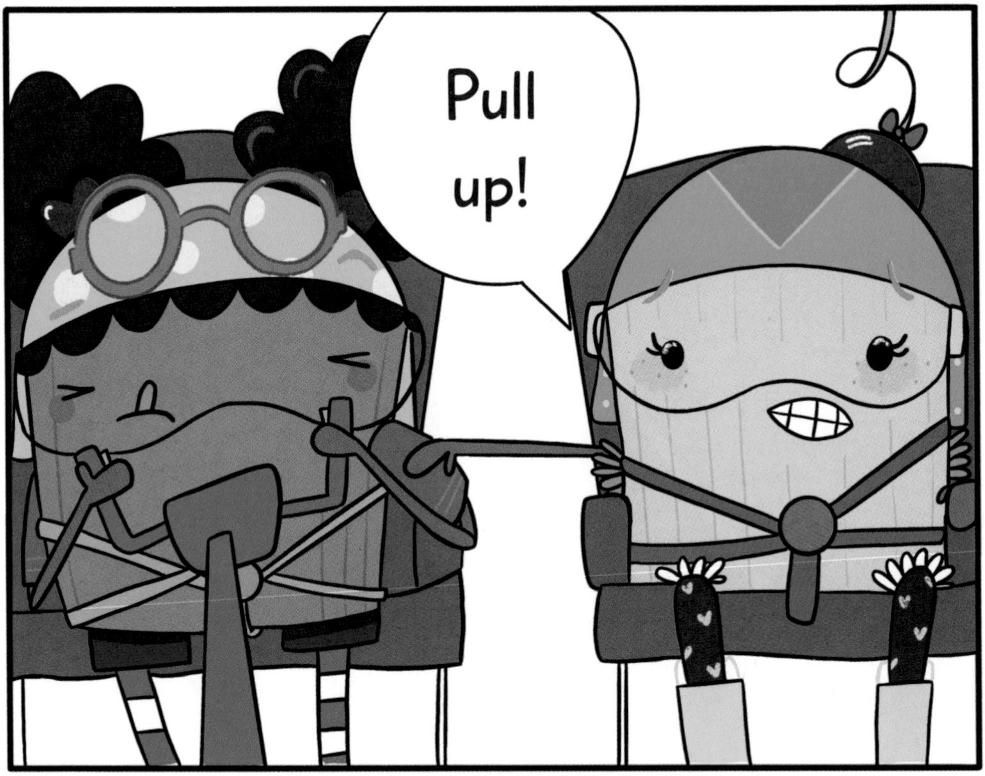
Pull up!
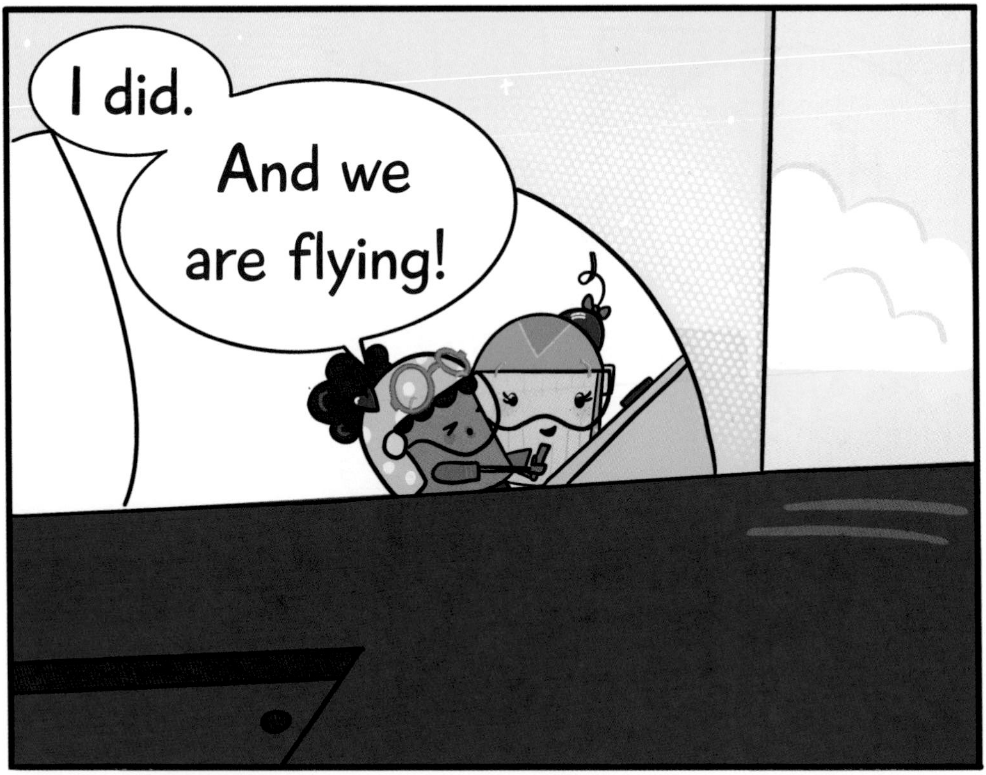
I did.
And we are flying!

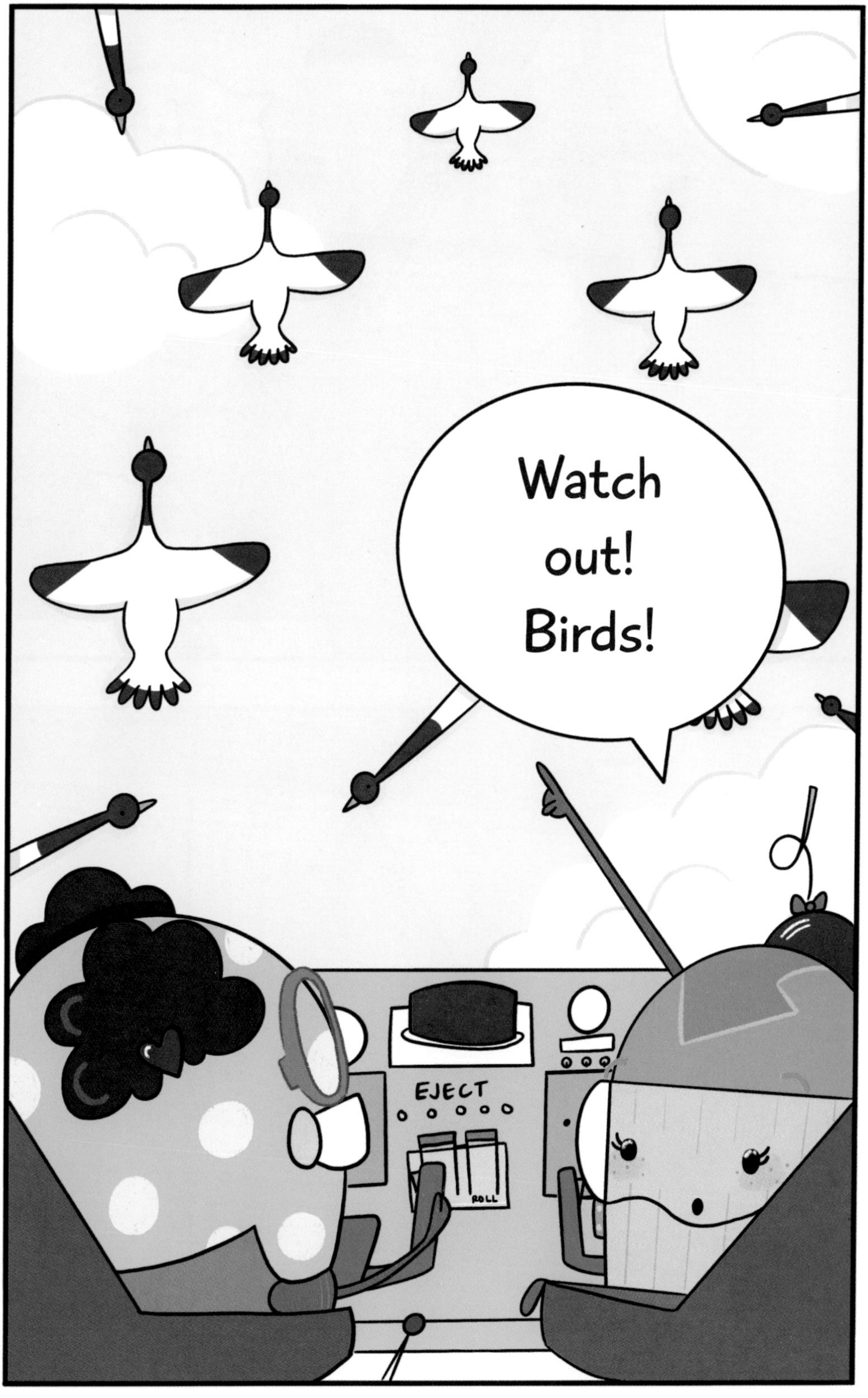
Watch out! Birds!
EJECT
ROLL

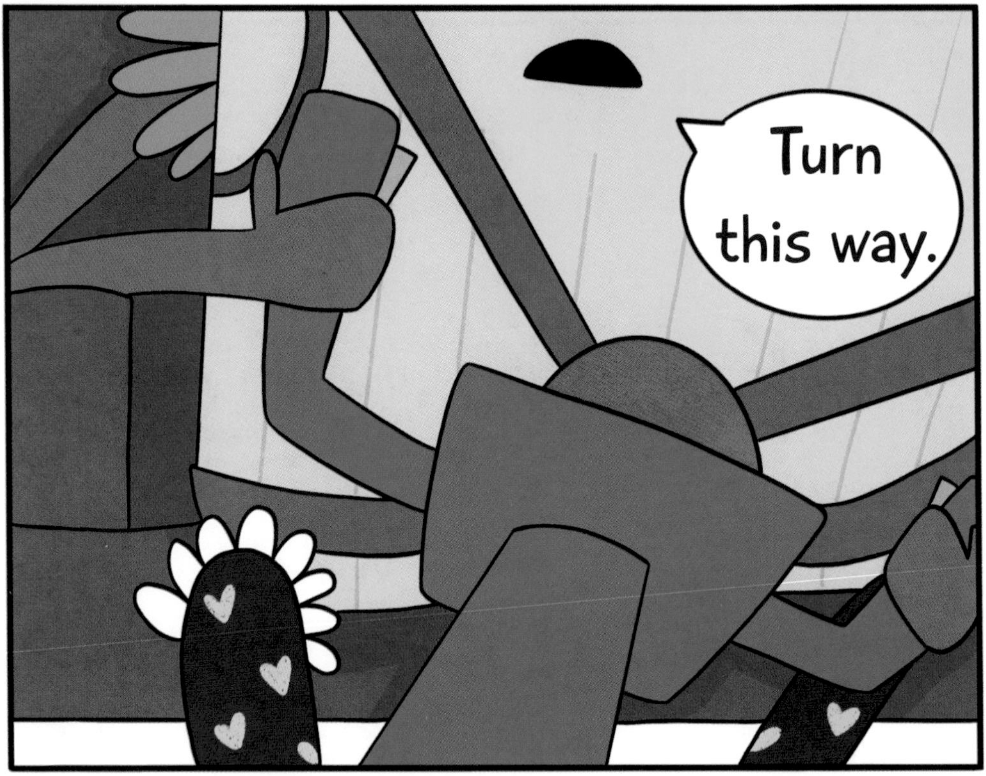
Turn this way.

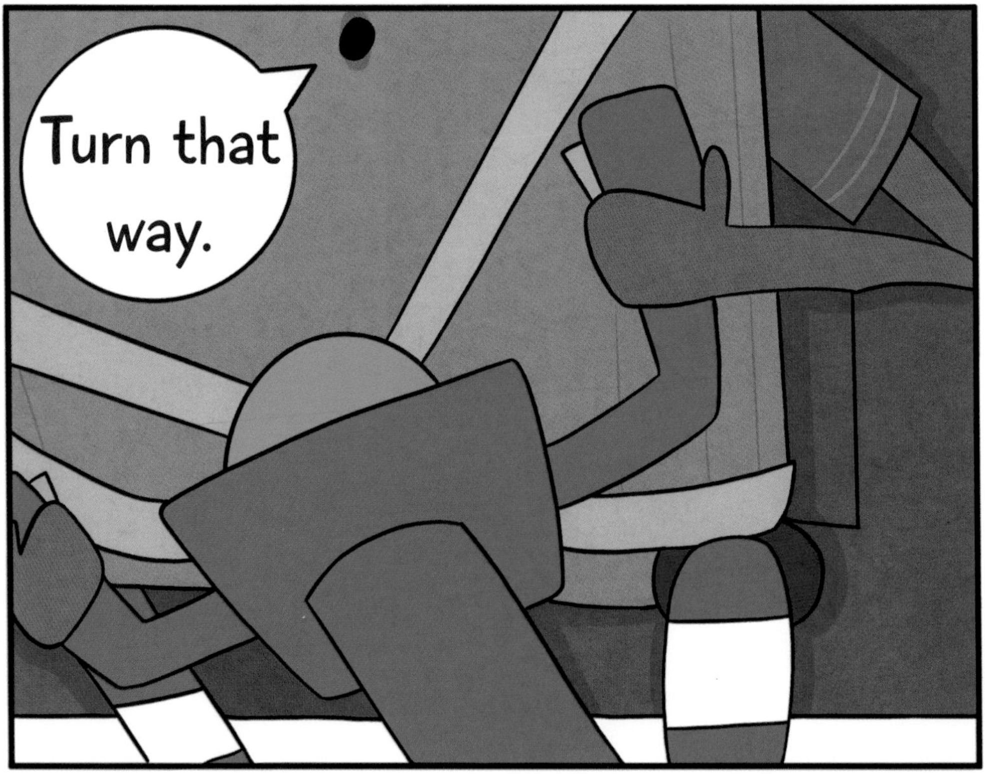
Turn that way.

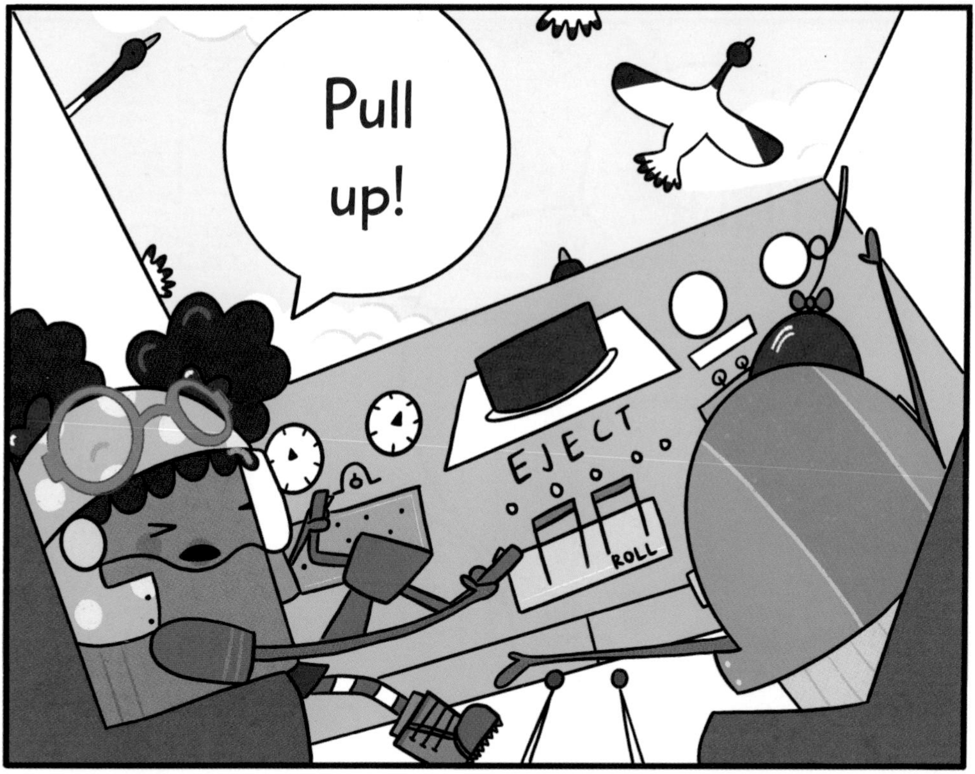
Pull up!
EJECT
ROLL

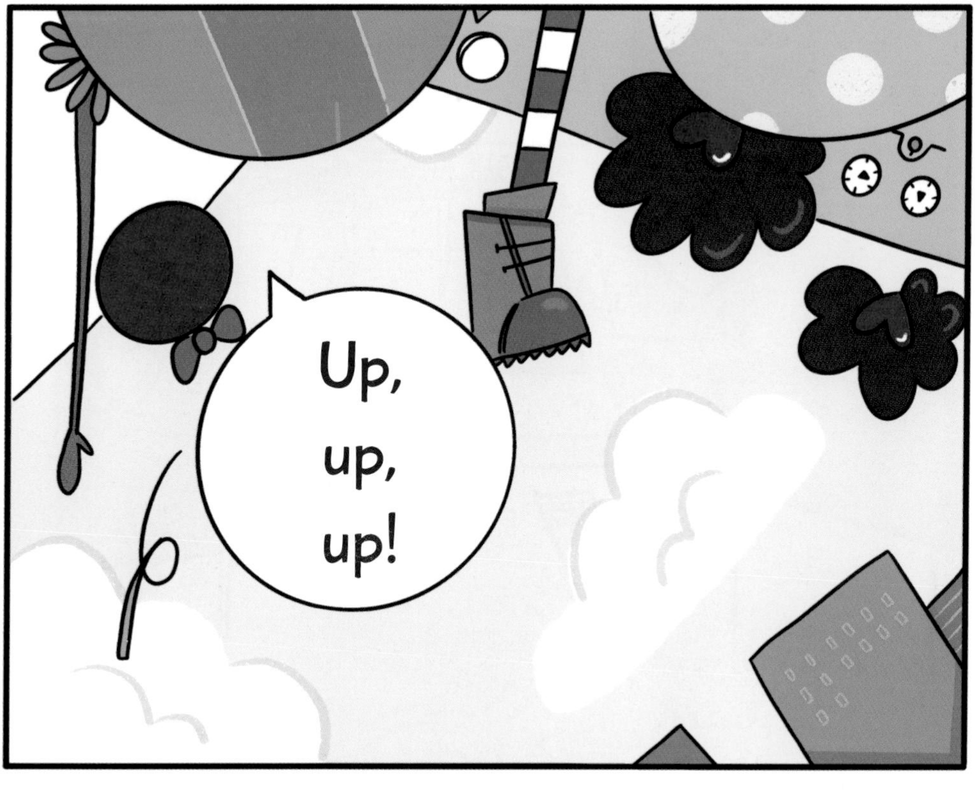
Up, up, up!

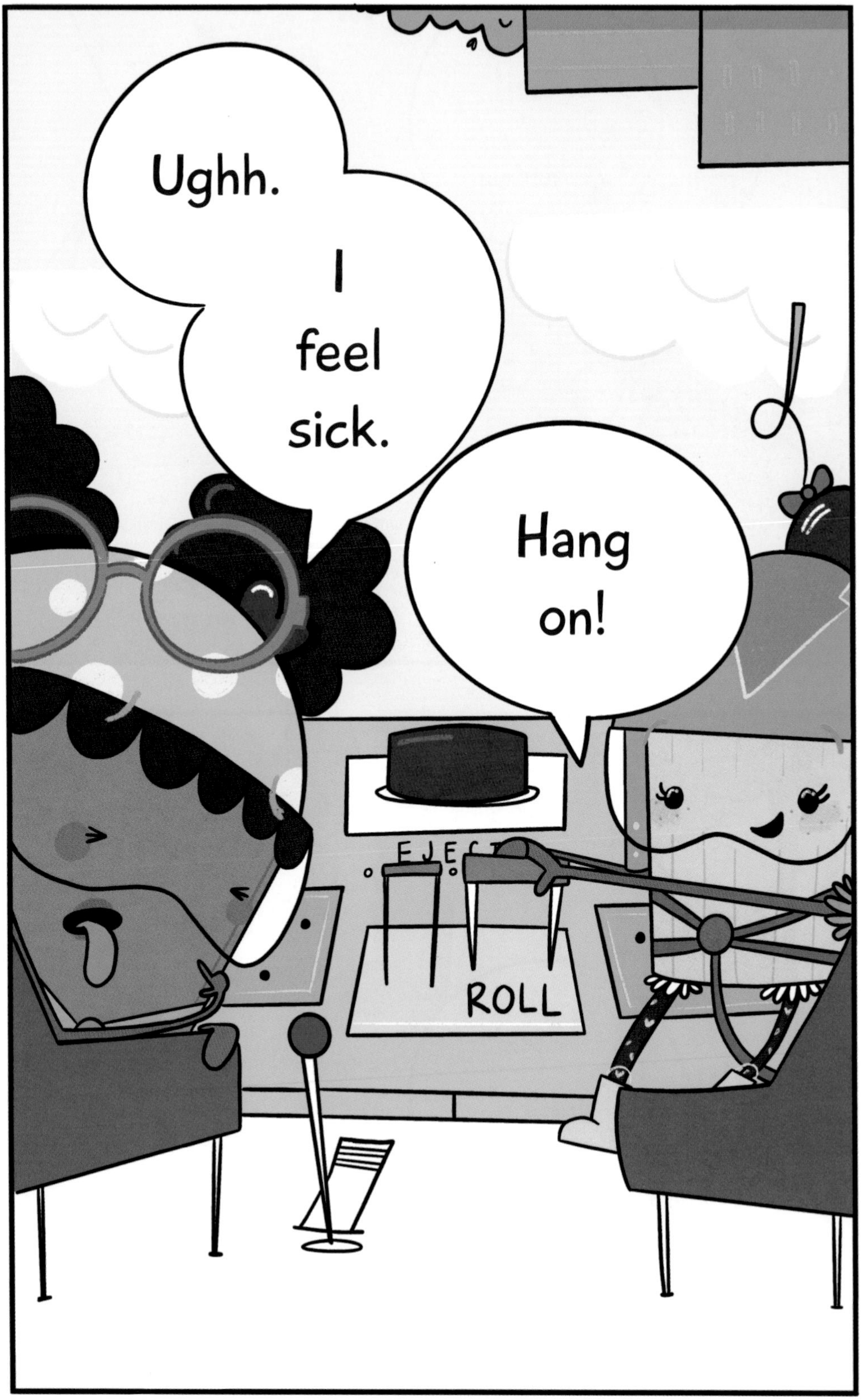
Ughh.
I feel sick.
Hang on!
EJECT
ROLL

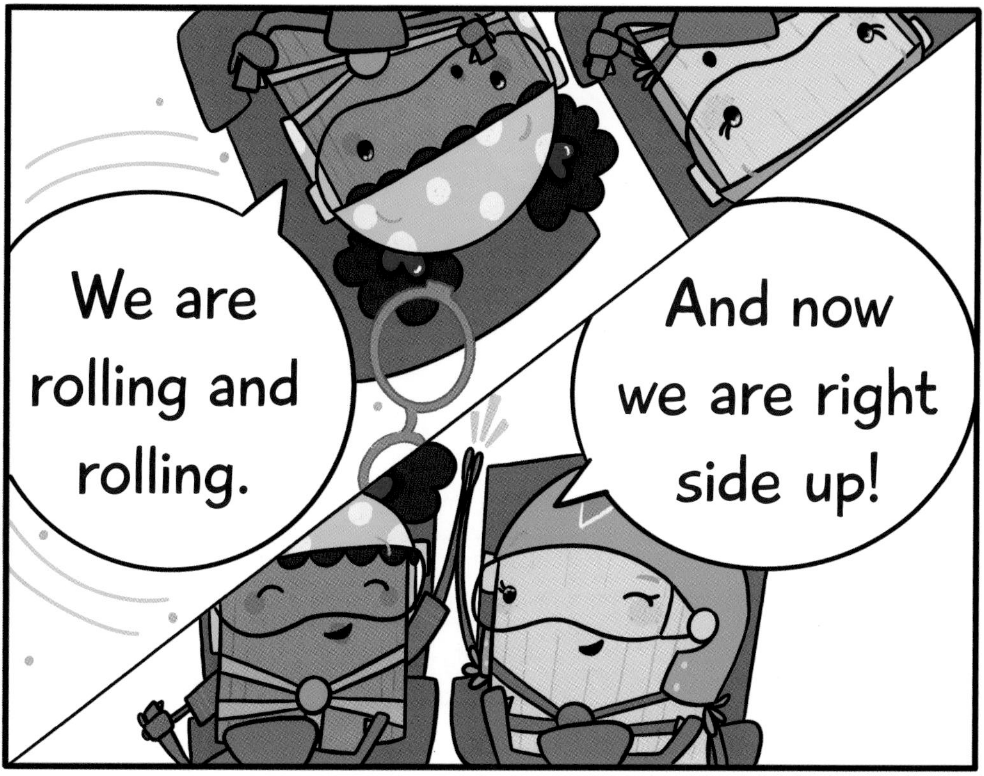
We are rolling and rolling.
And now we are right side up!

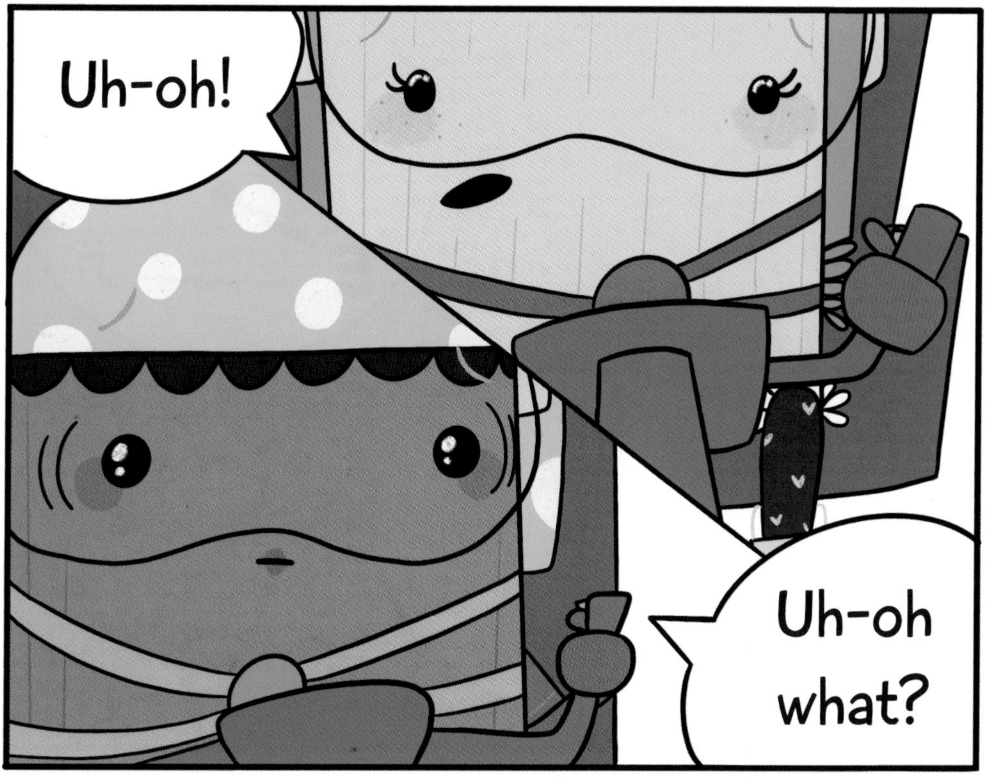
Uh-oh!
Uh-oh what?

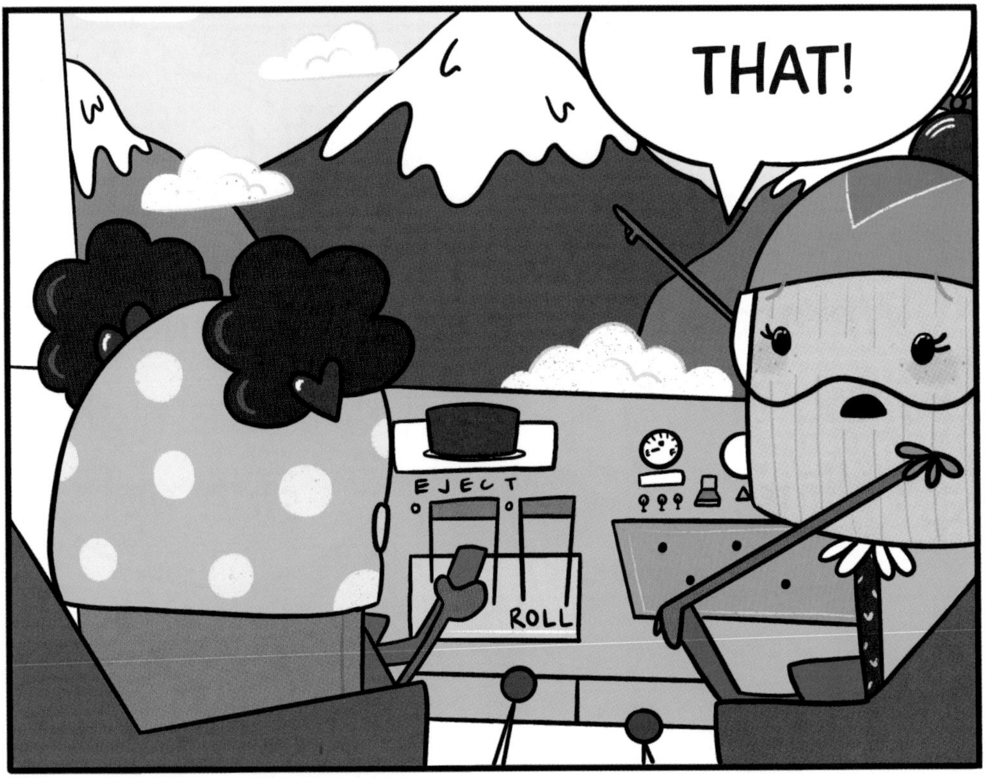
THAT!
EJECT
ROLL

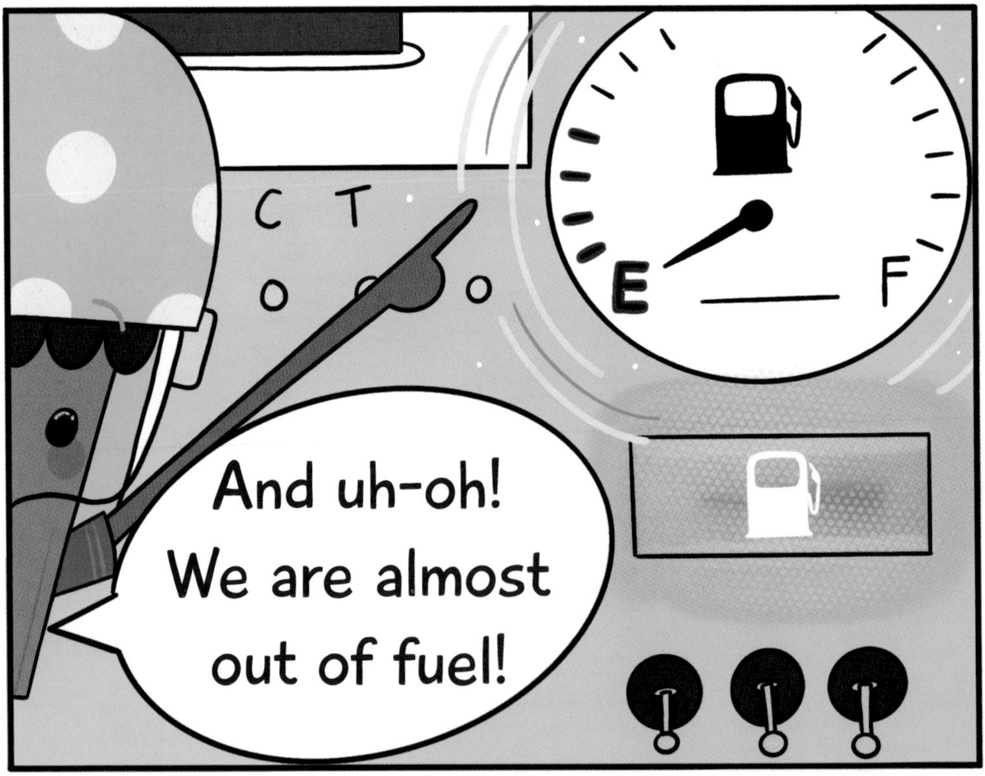
C T
E
F
And uh-oh! We are almost out of fuel!

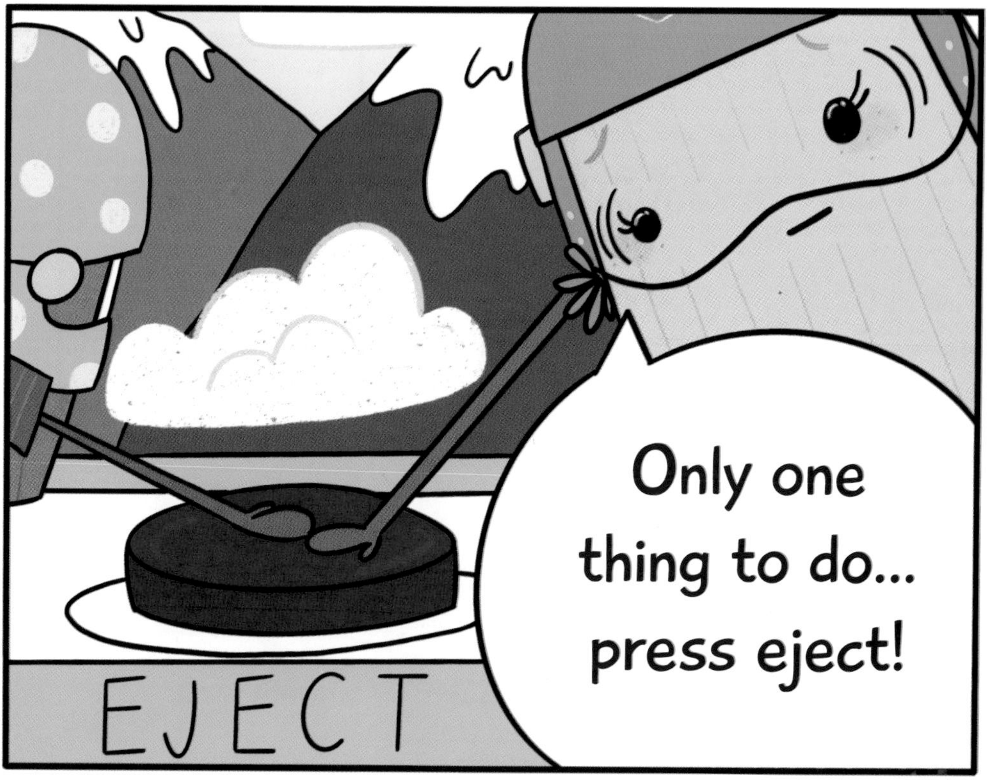
EJECT
Only one thing to do... press eject!

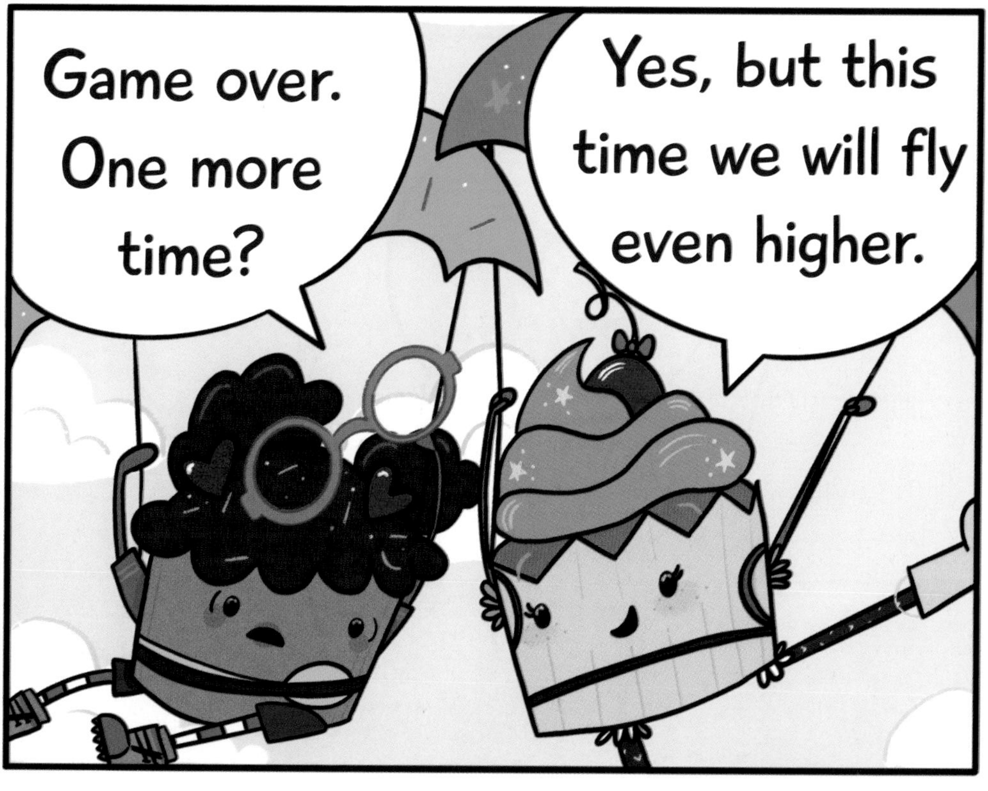
Game over. One more time?
Yes, but this time we will fly even higher.

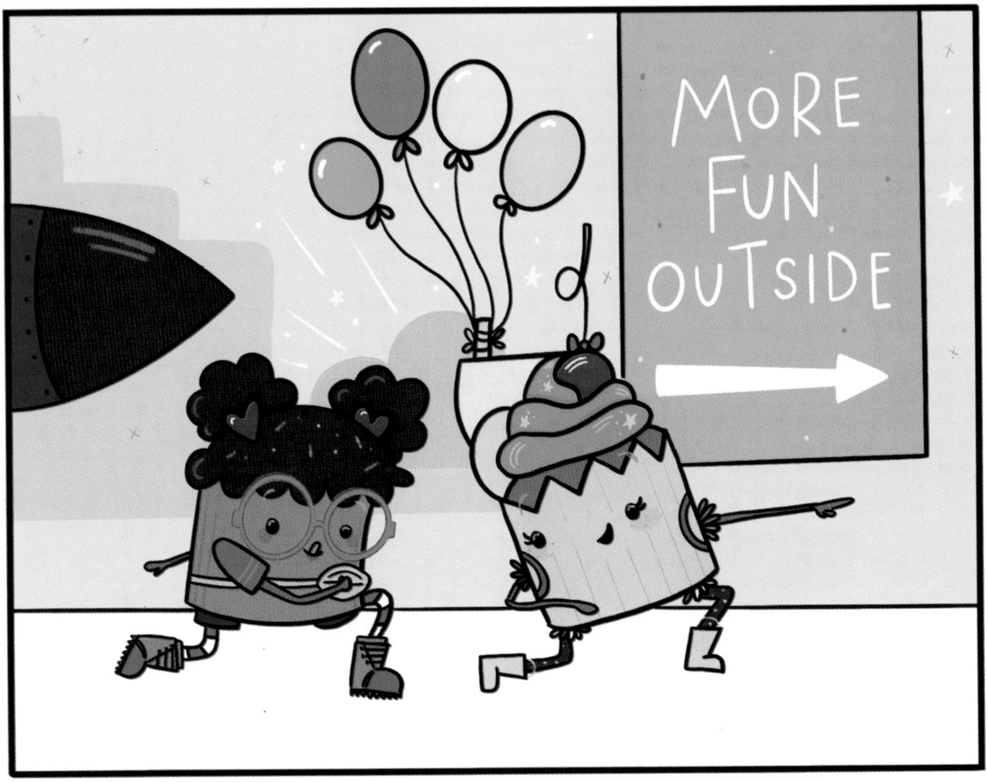
MORE FUN OUTSIDE

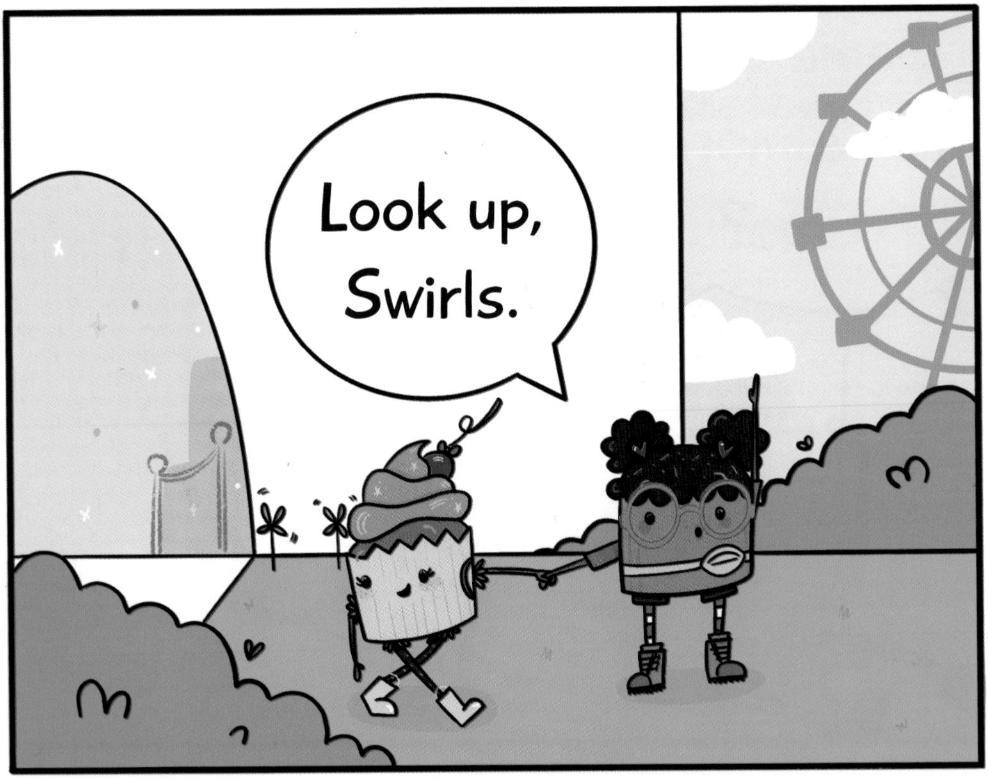
Look up, Swirls.

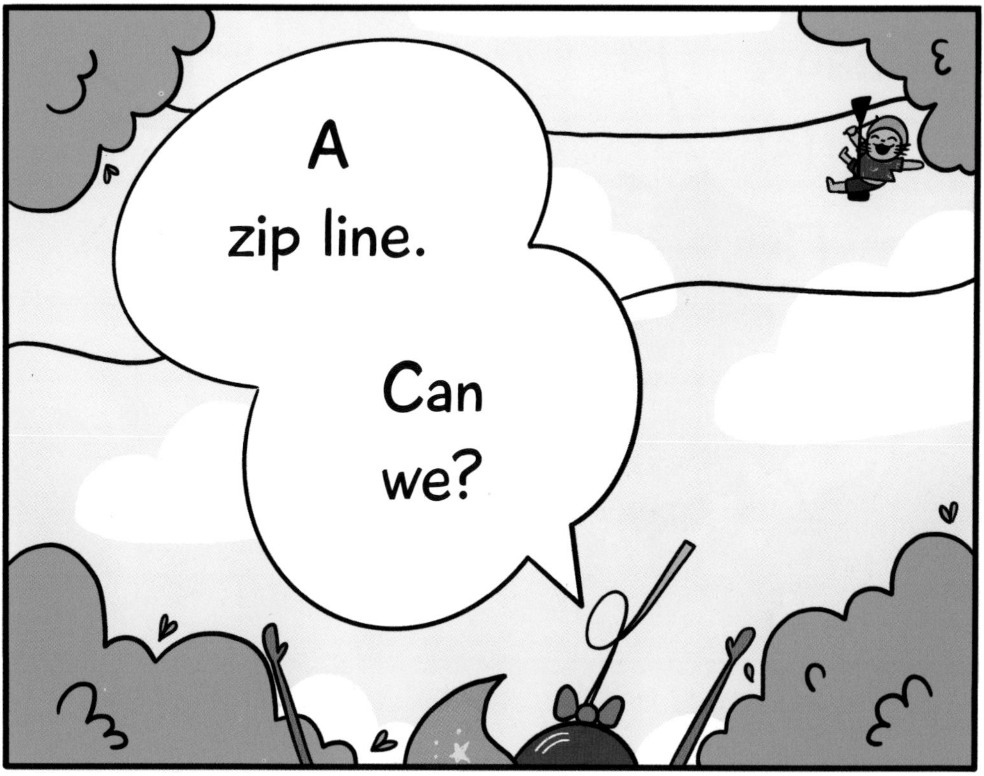
A zip line.
Can we?

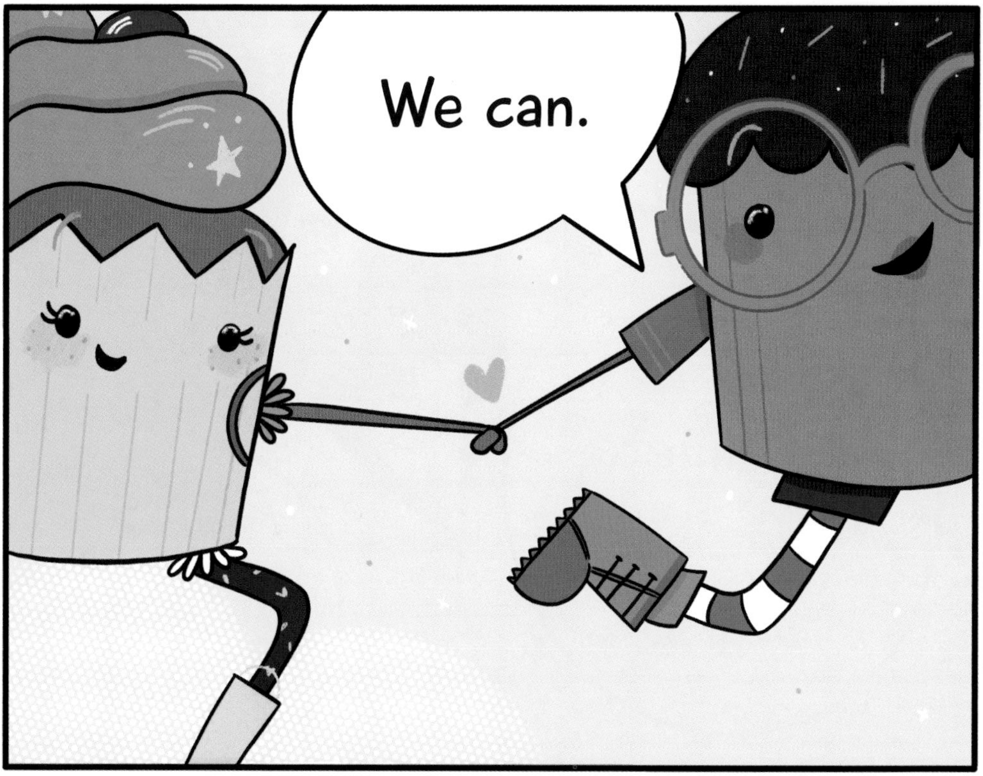
We can.

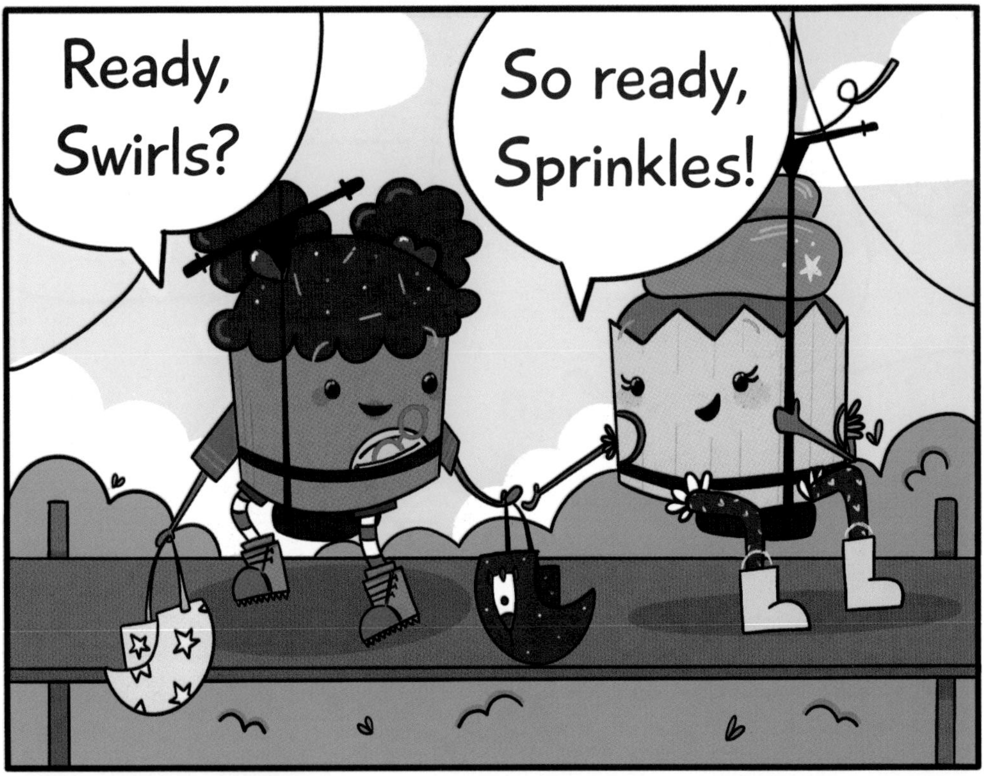
Ready, Swirls?
So ready, Sprinkles!

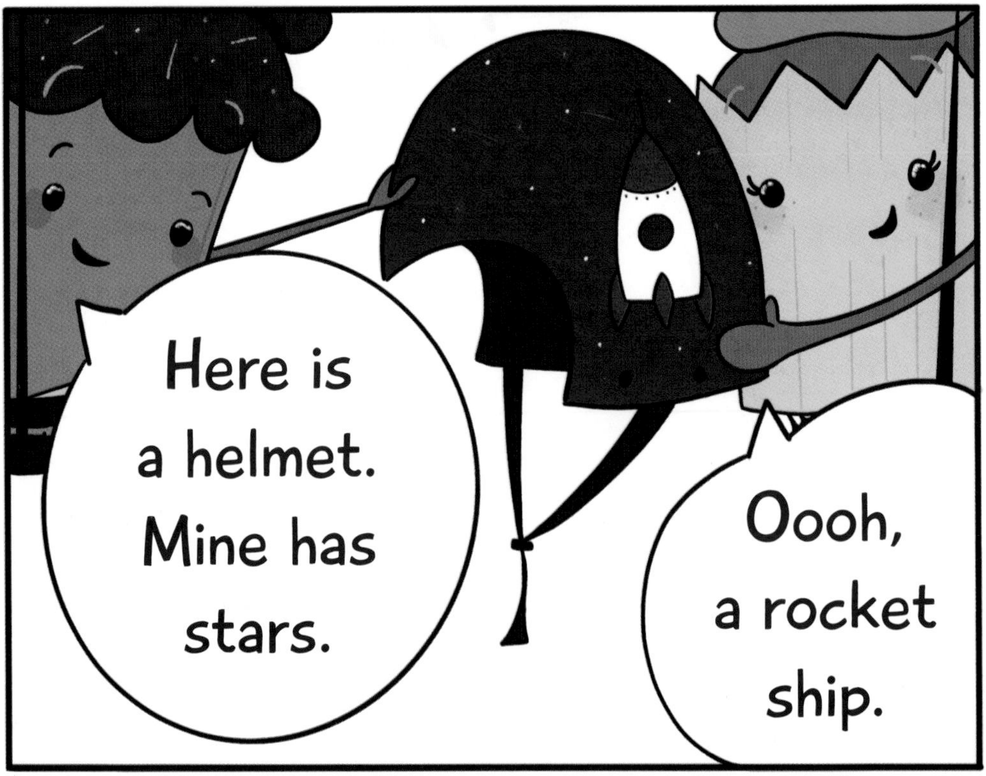
Here is a helmet. Mine has stars.
Oooh, a rocket ship.

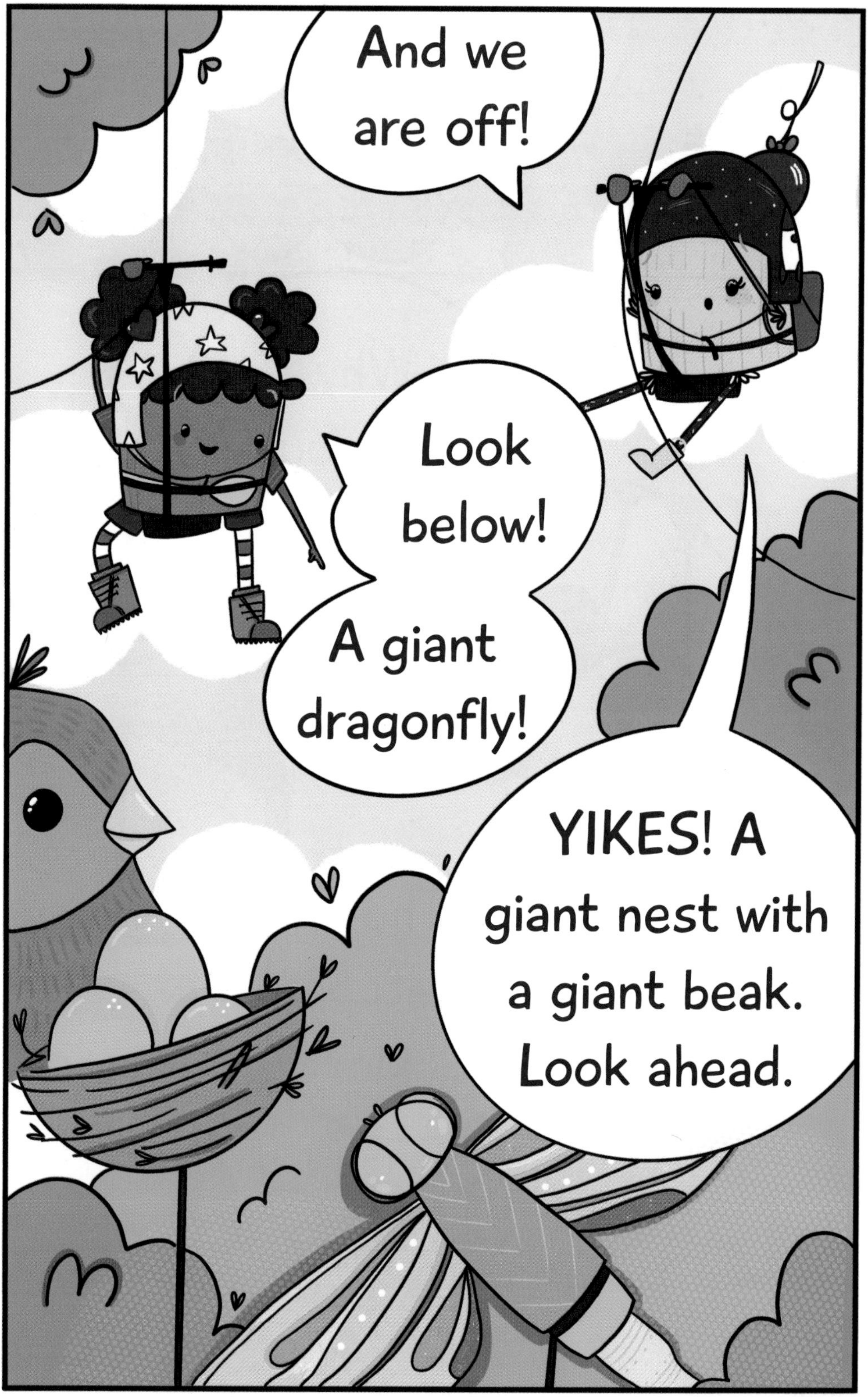
And we are off!
Look below!
A giant dragonfly!
YIKES! A giant nest with a giant beak. Look ahead.

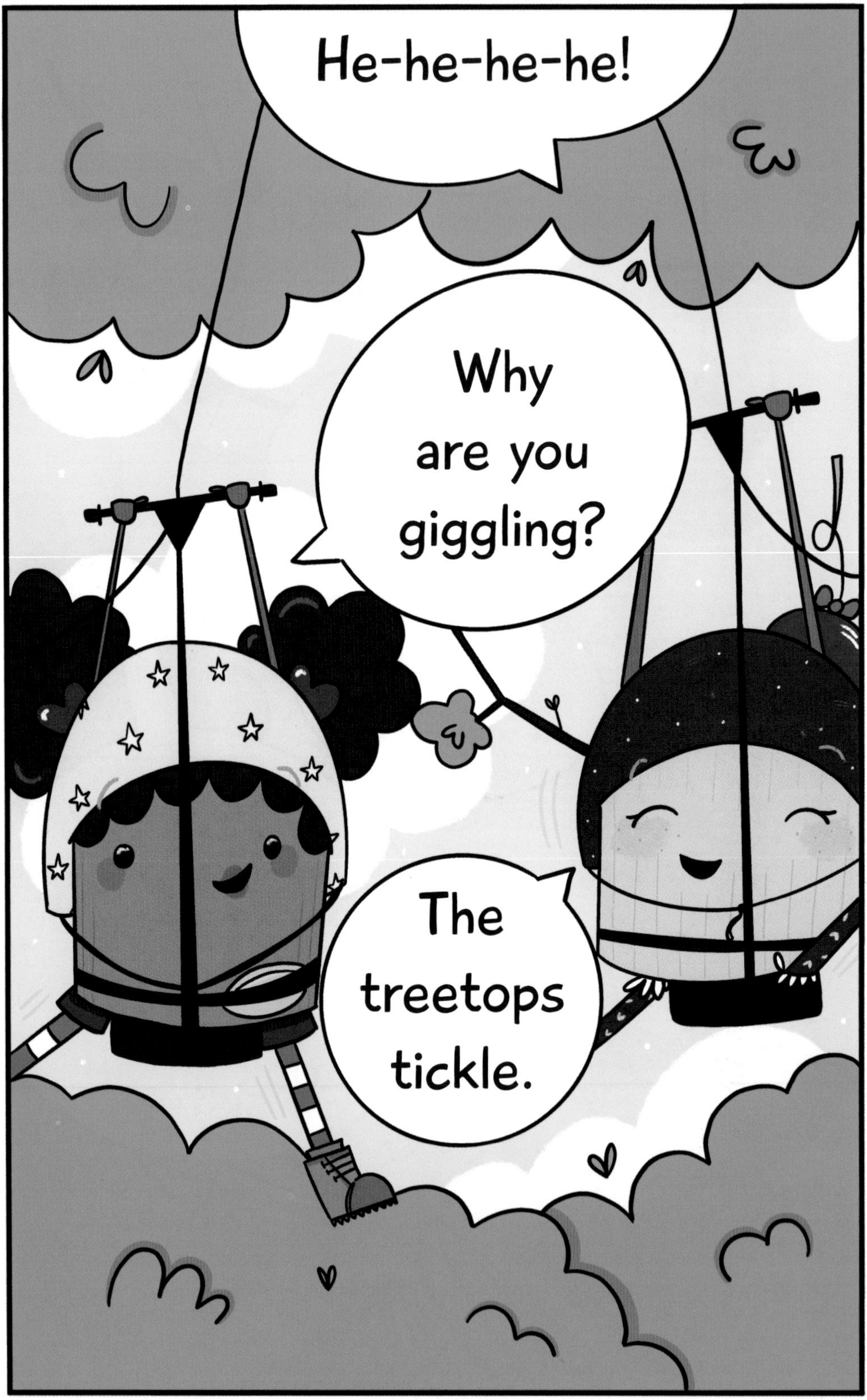
He-he-he-he!
Why are you giggling?
The treetops tickle.

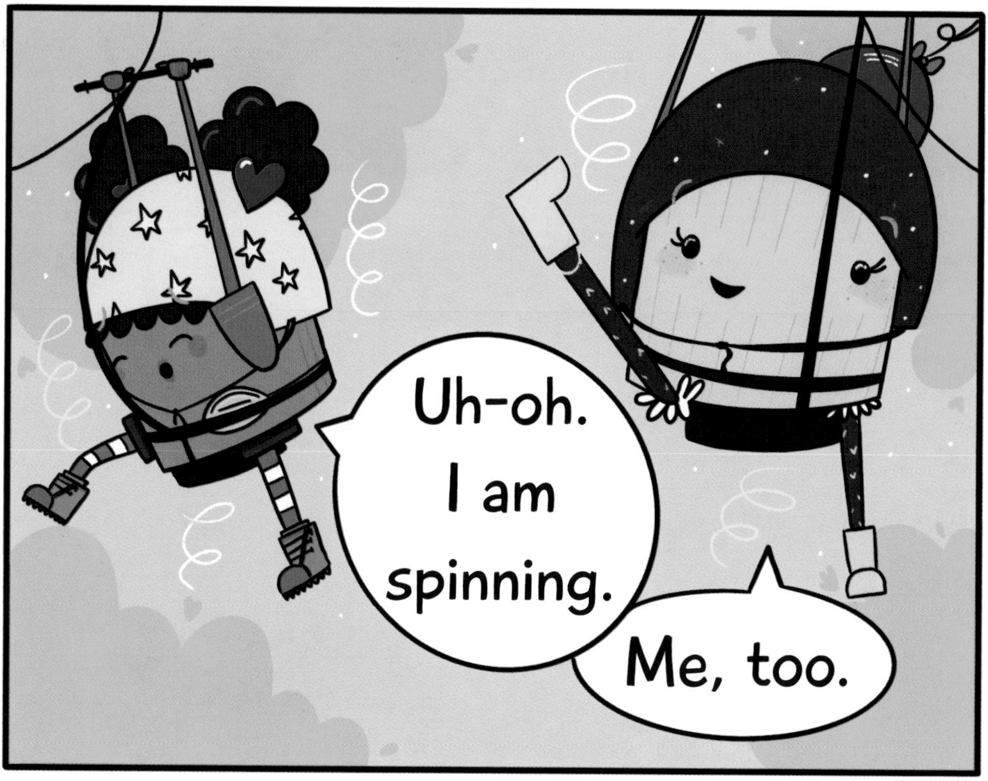
Uh-oh. I am spinning.
Me, too.

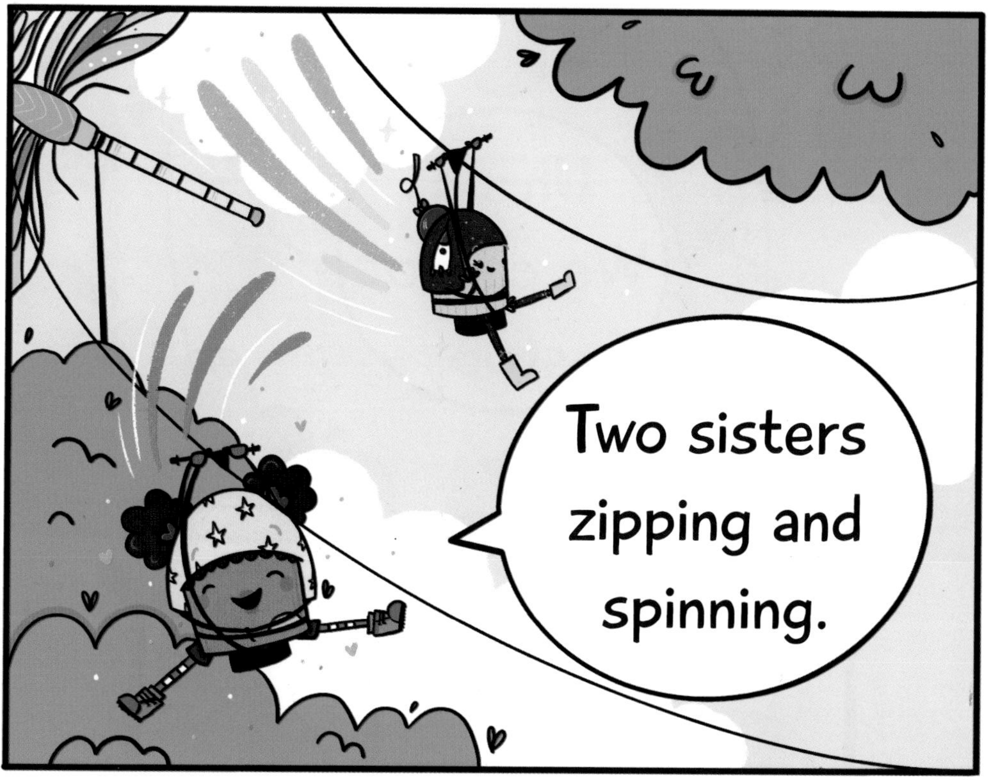
Two sisters zipping and spinning.

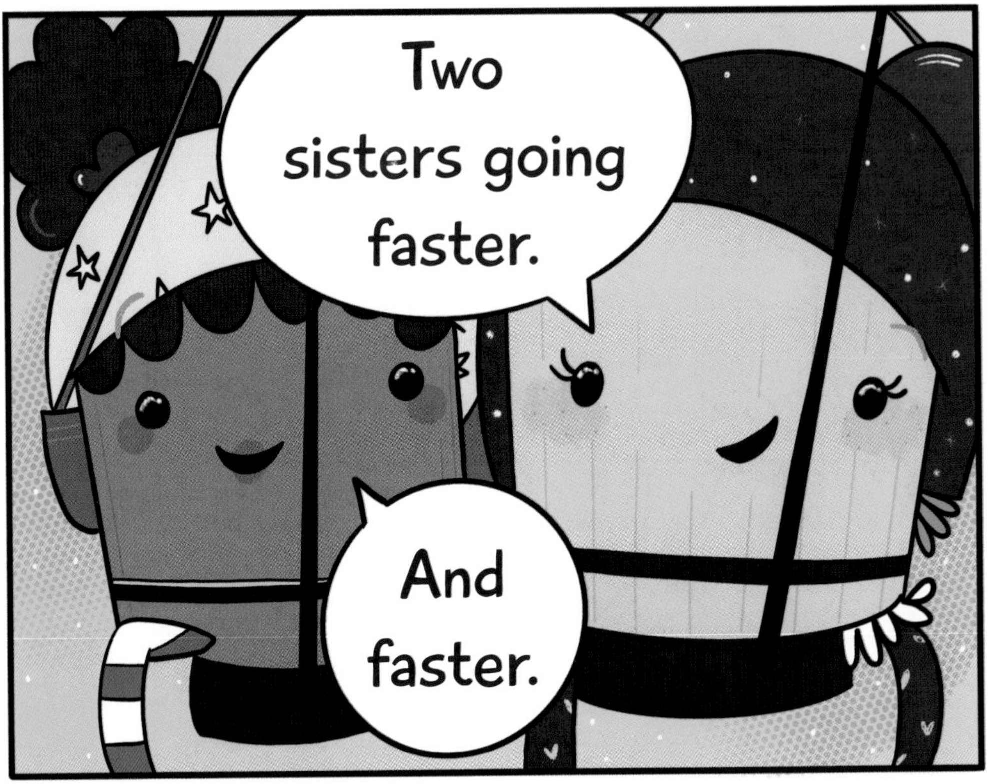
Two sisters going faster.
And faster.

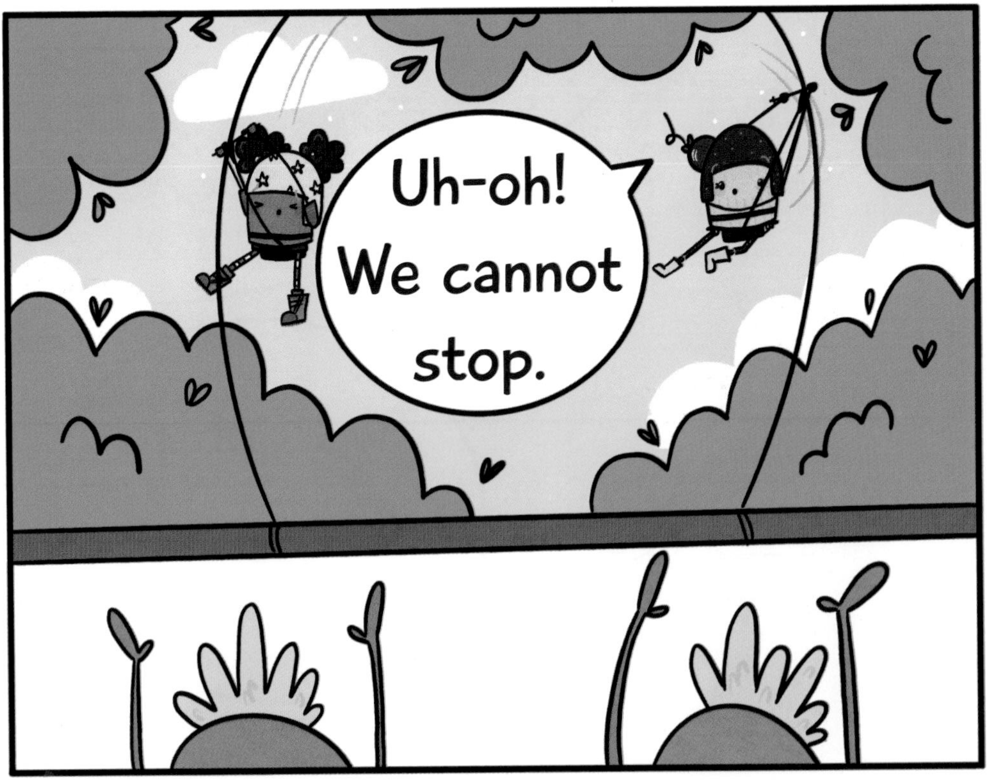
Uh-oh! We cannot stop.

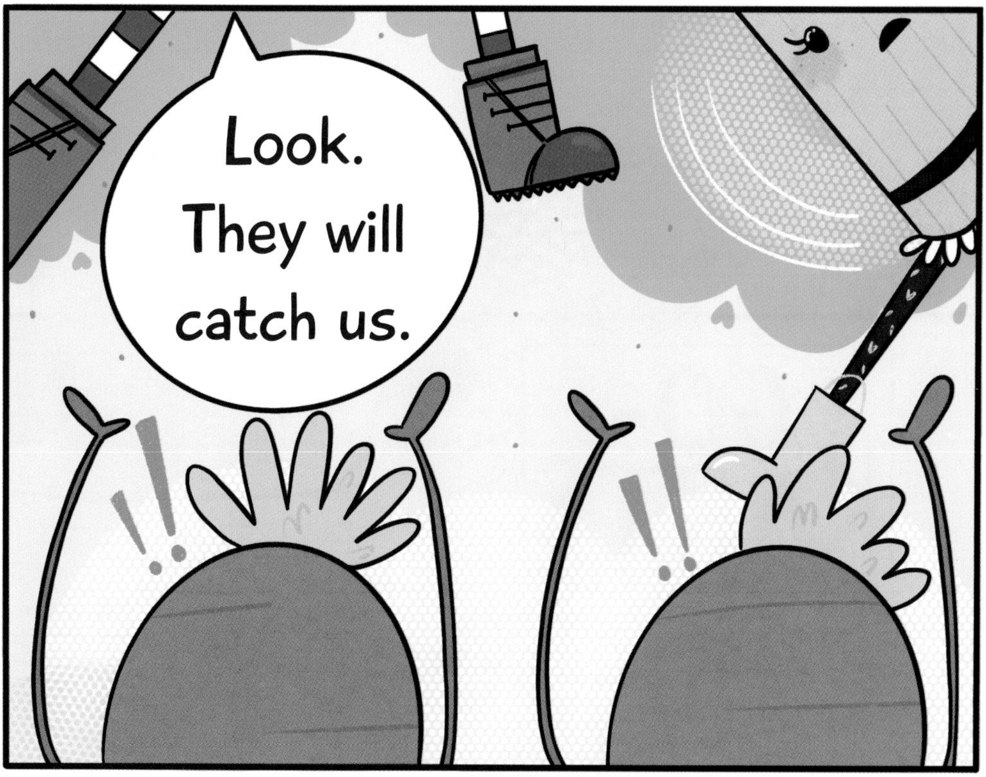
Look. They will catch us.

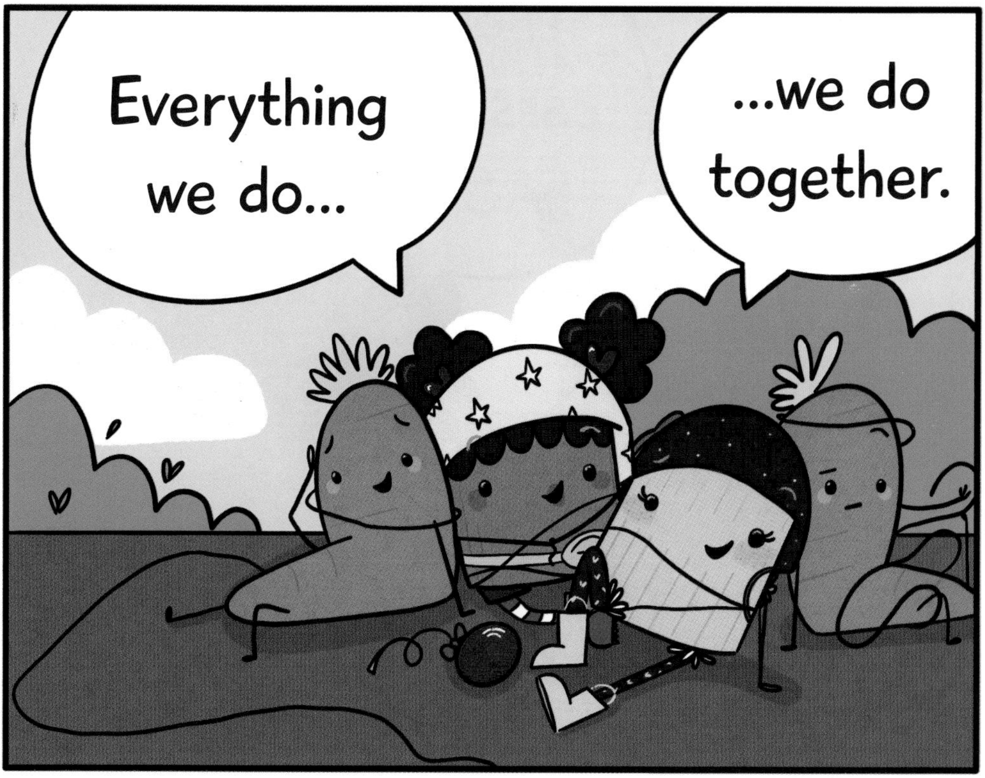
Everything we do...
...we do together.

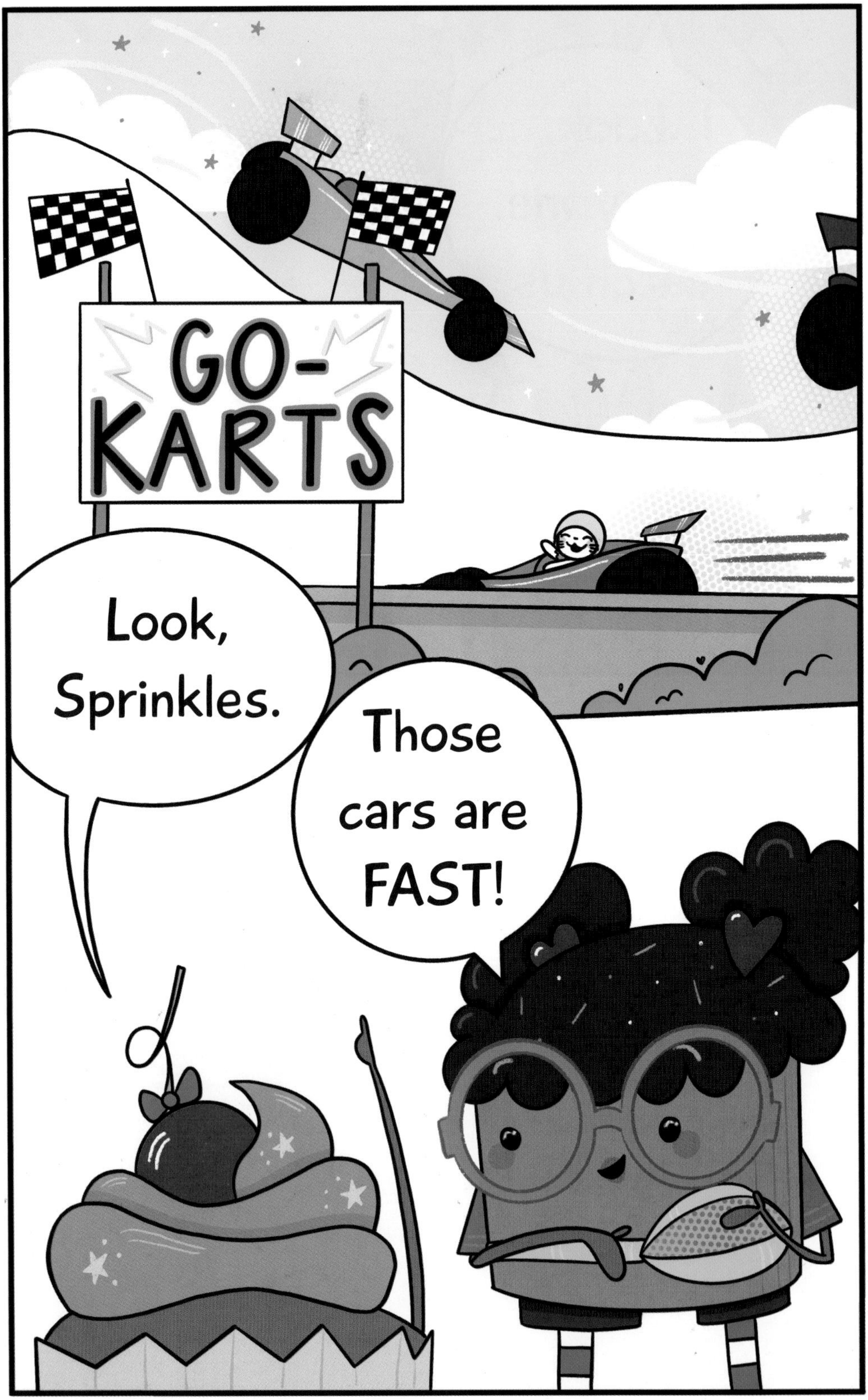
GO-KARTS
Look, Sprinkles.
Those cars are FAST!

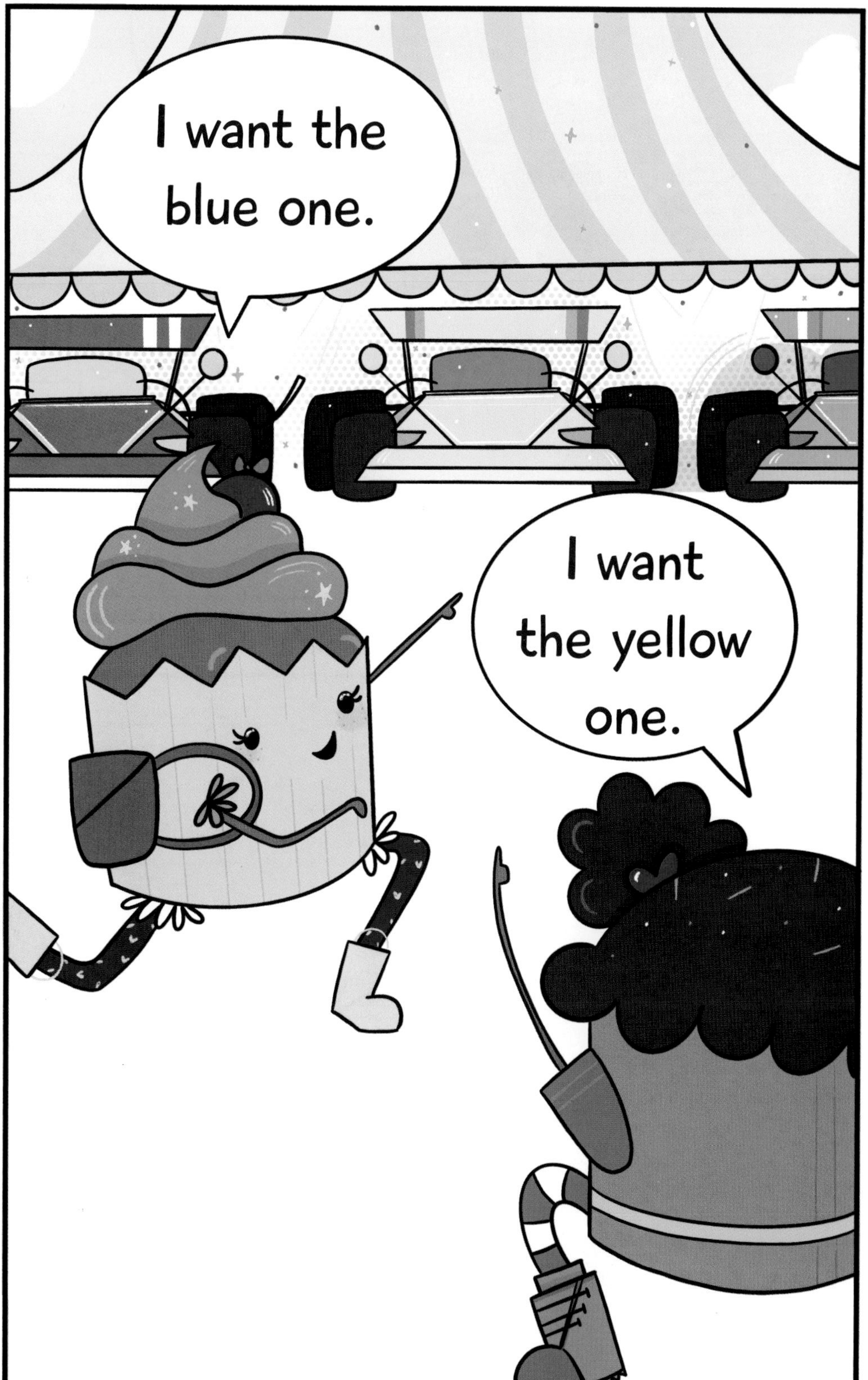
I want the blue one.
I want the yellow one.

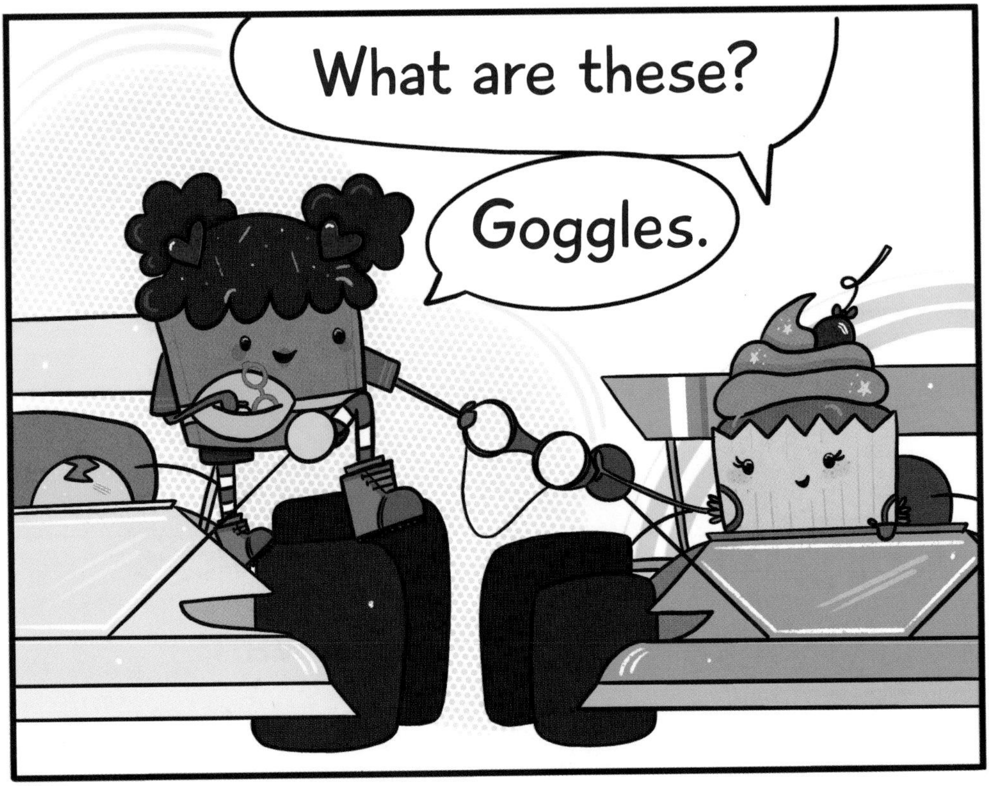
What are these?
Goggles.

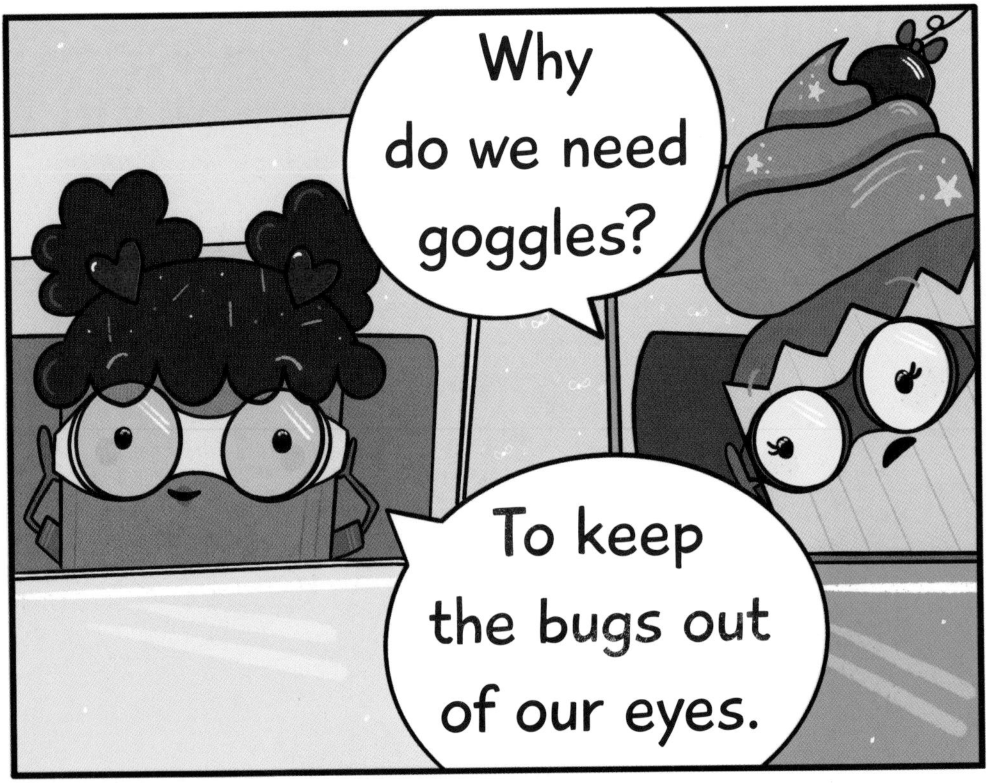
Why do we need goggles?
To keep the bugs out of our eyes.

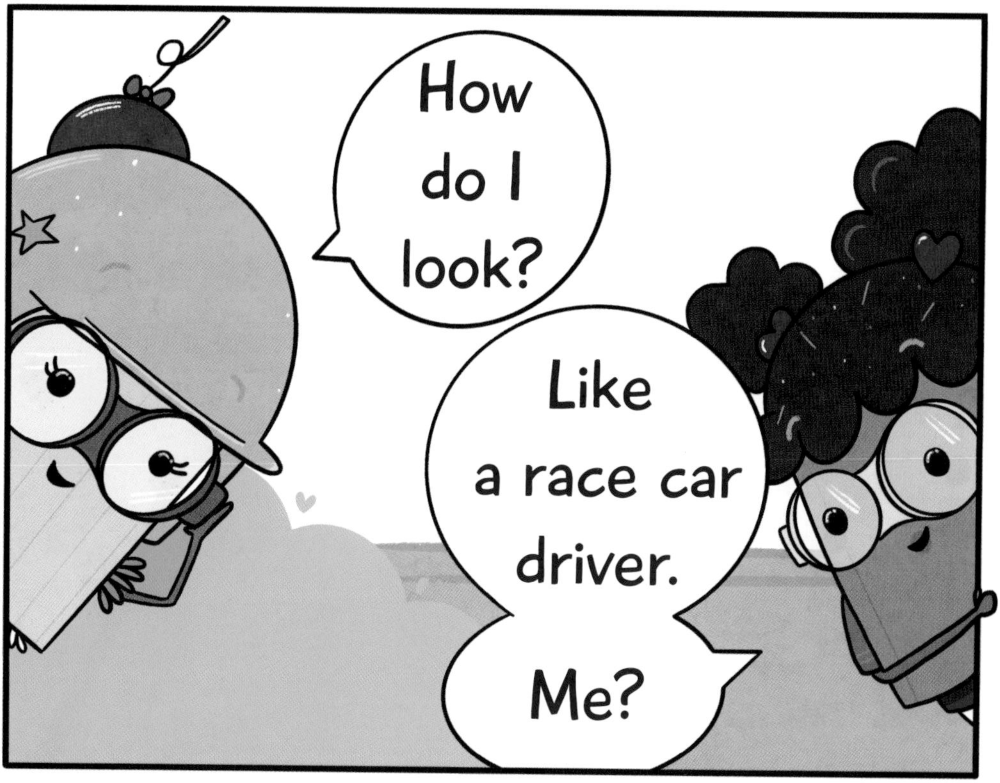
How do I look?
Like a race car driver.
Me?
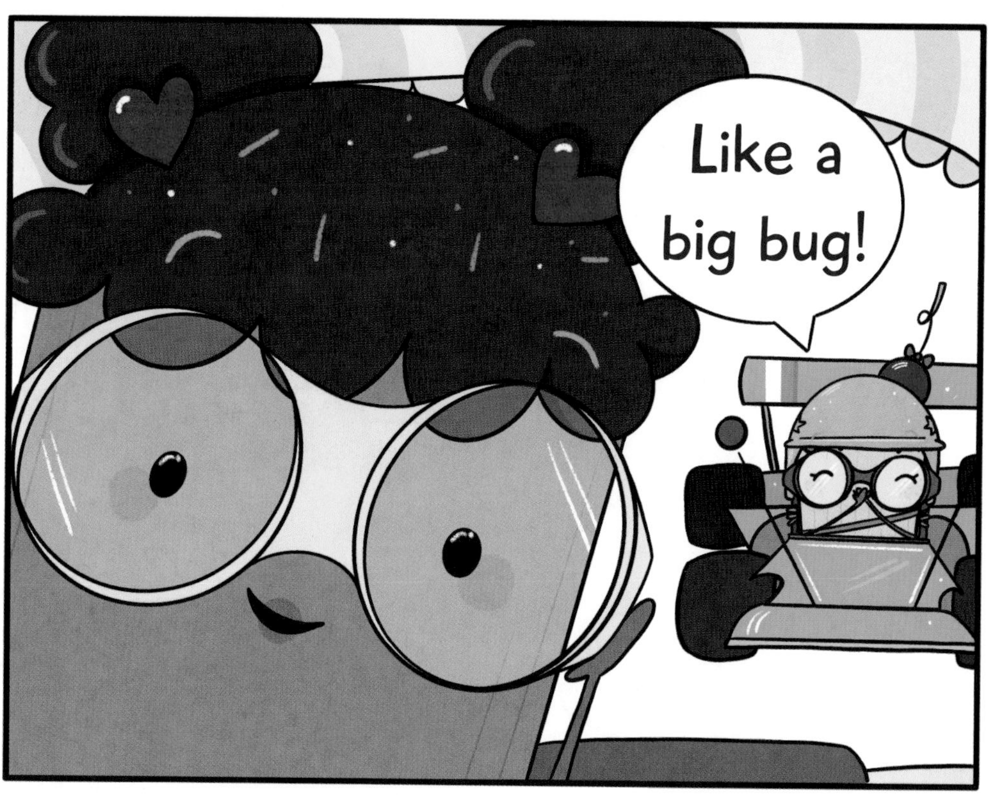
Like a big bug!

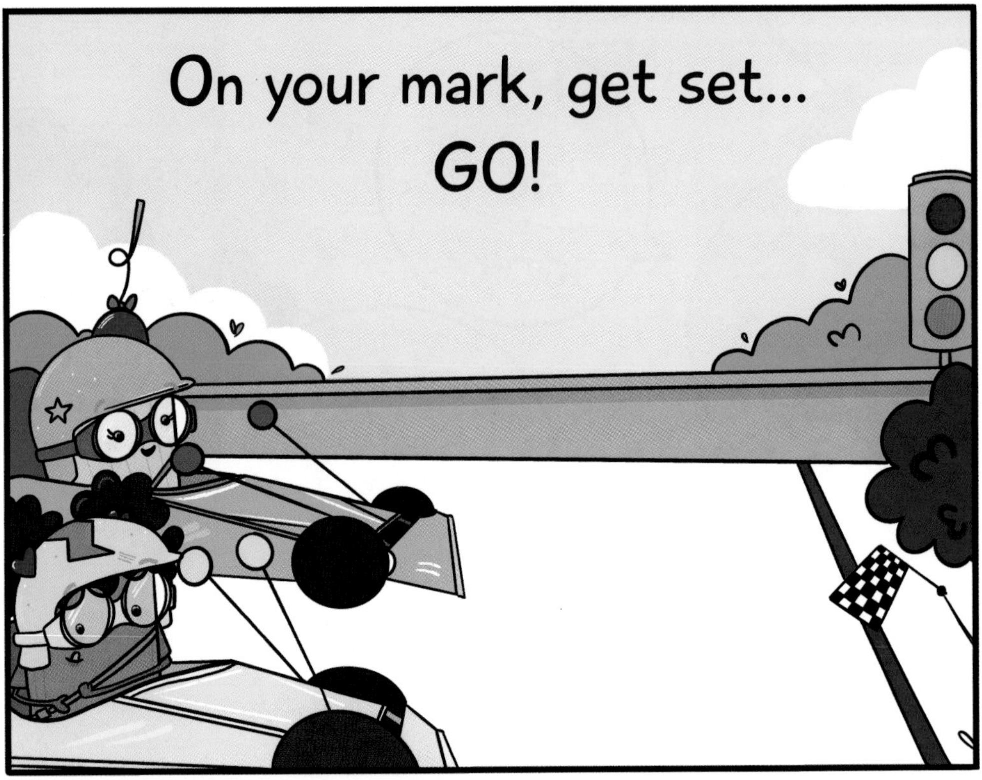
On your mark, get set...
GO!

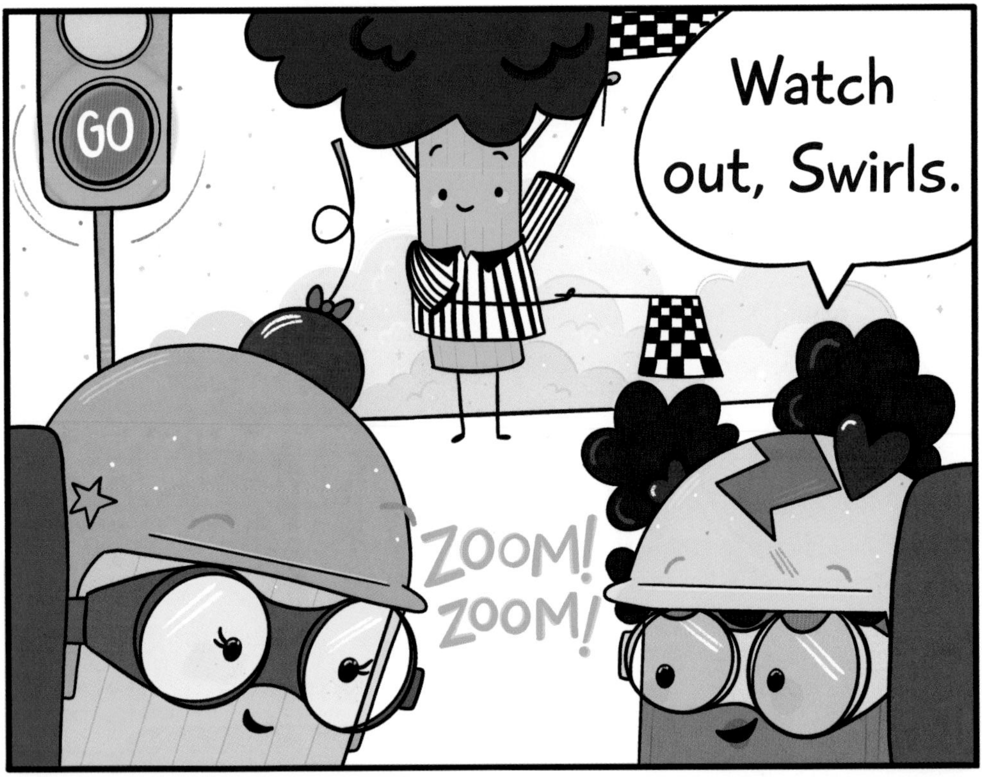
GO
Watch out, Swirls.
ZOOM!
ZOOM!

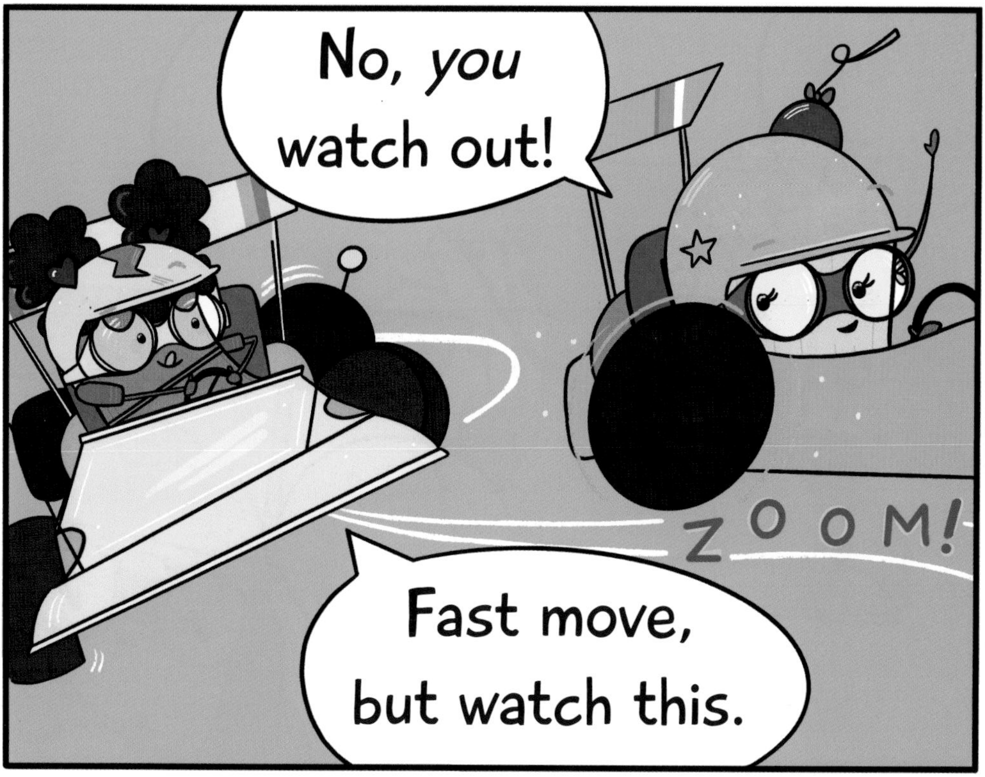
No, *you* watch out!
ZOOM!
Fast move, but watch this.

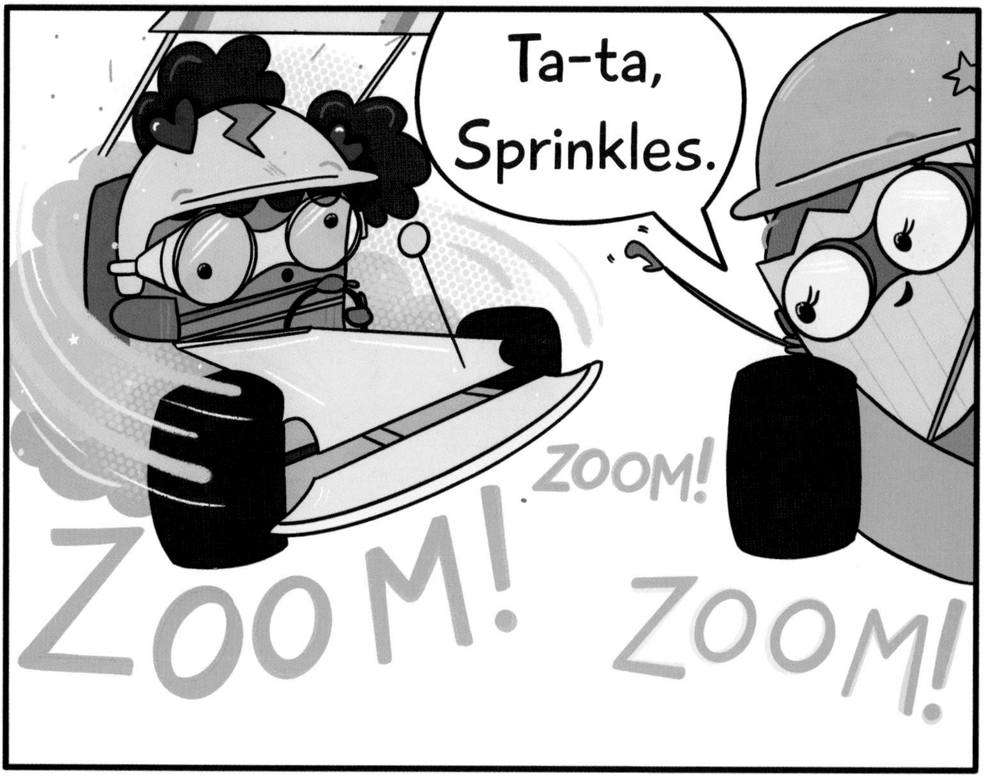
Ta-ta, Sprinkles.
ZOOM!
ZOOM!
ZOOM!

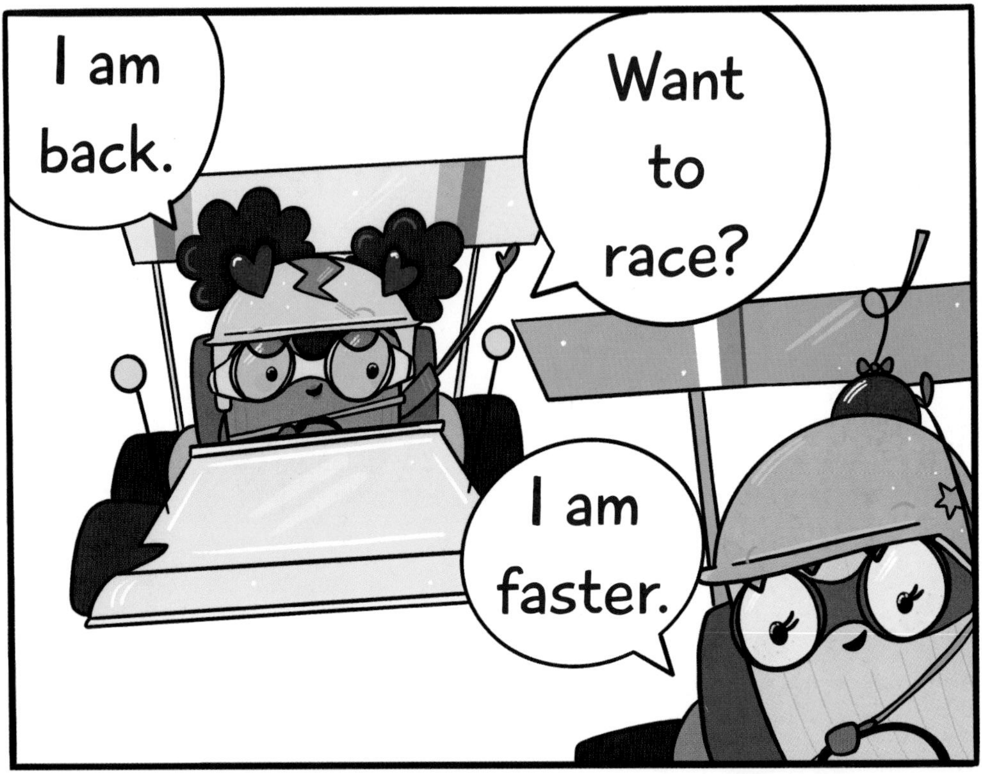
I am back.
Want to race?
I am faster.

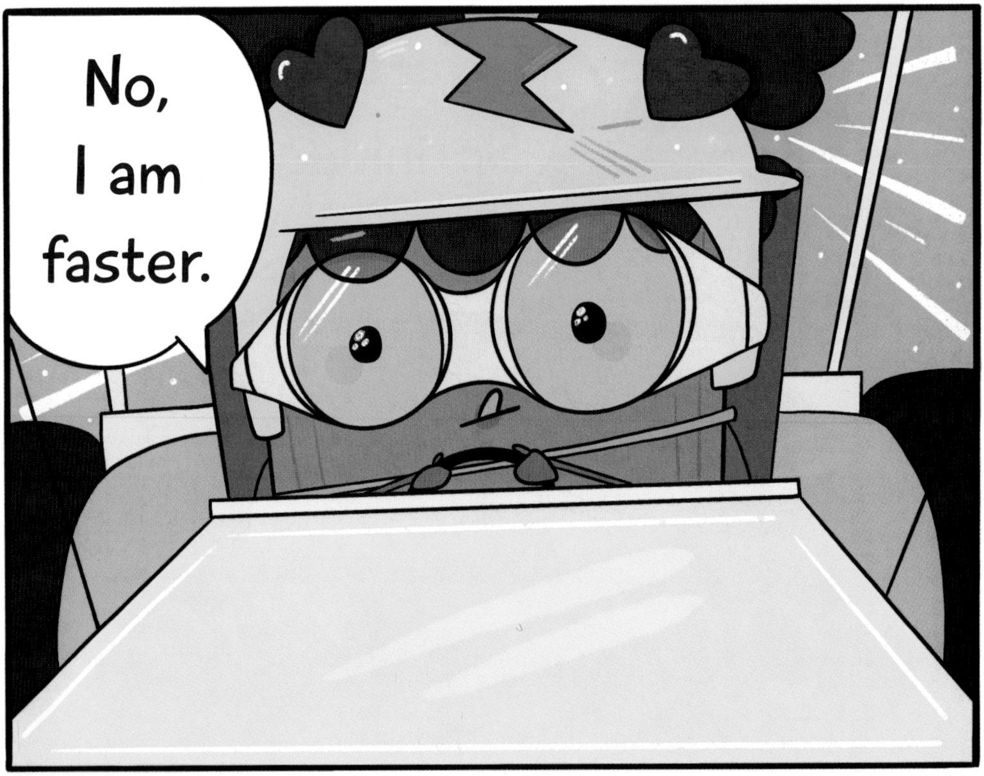
No, I am faster.

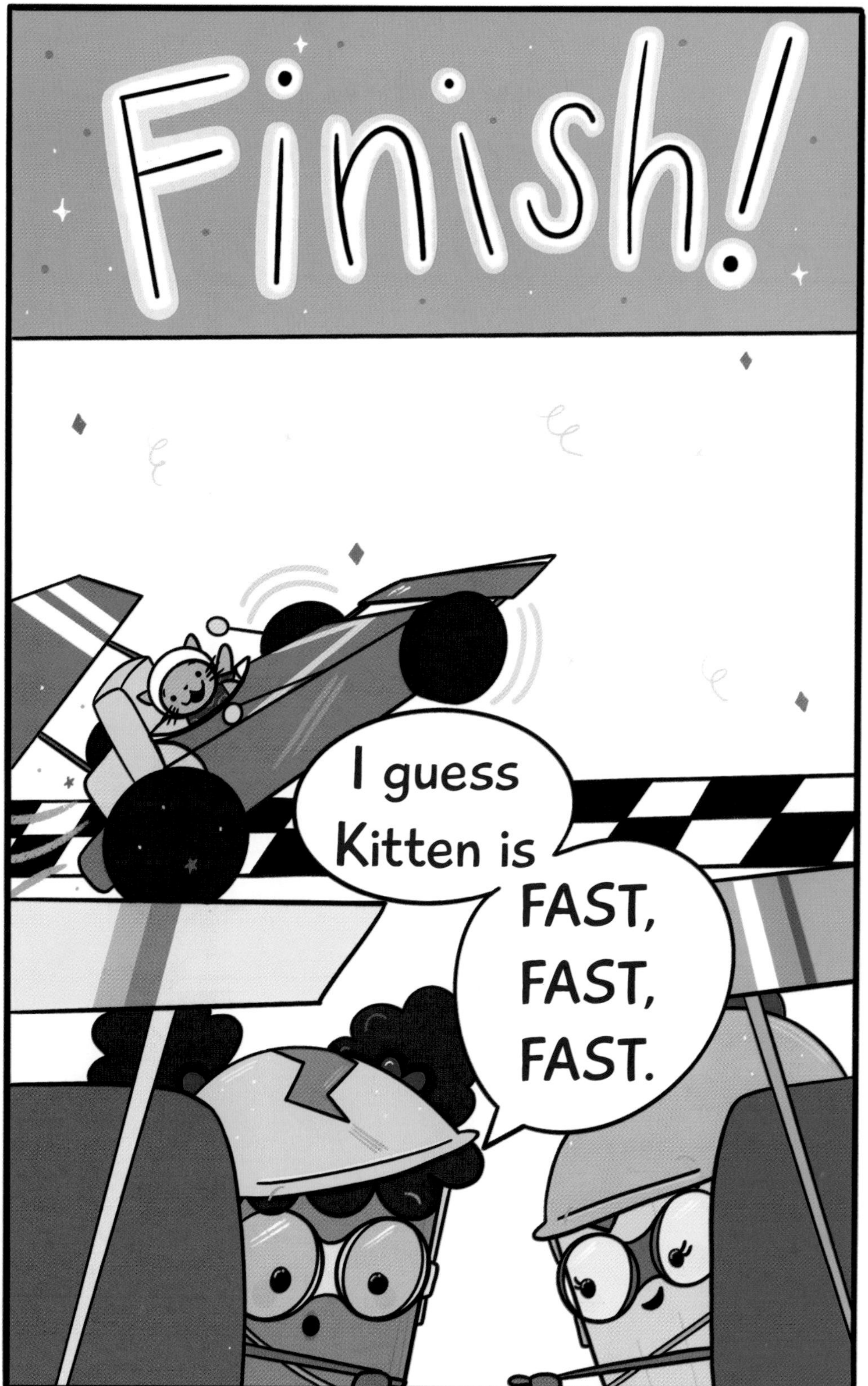
Finish!
I guess Kitten is
FAST, FAST, FAST.

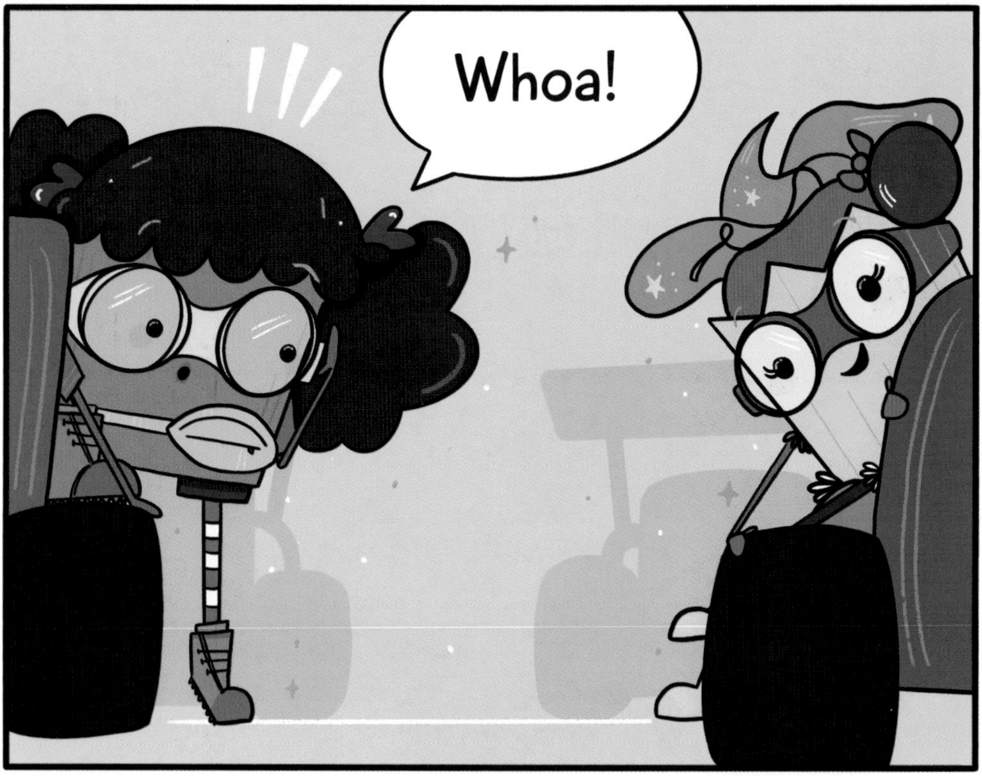
Whoa!

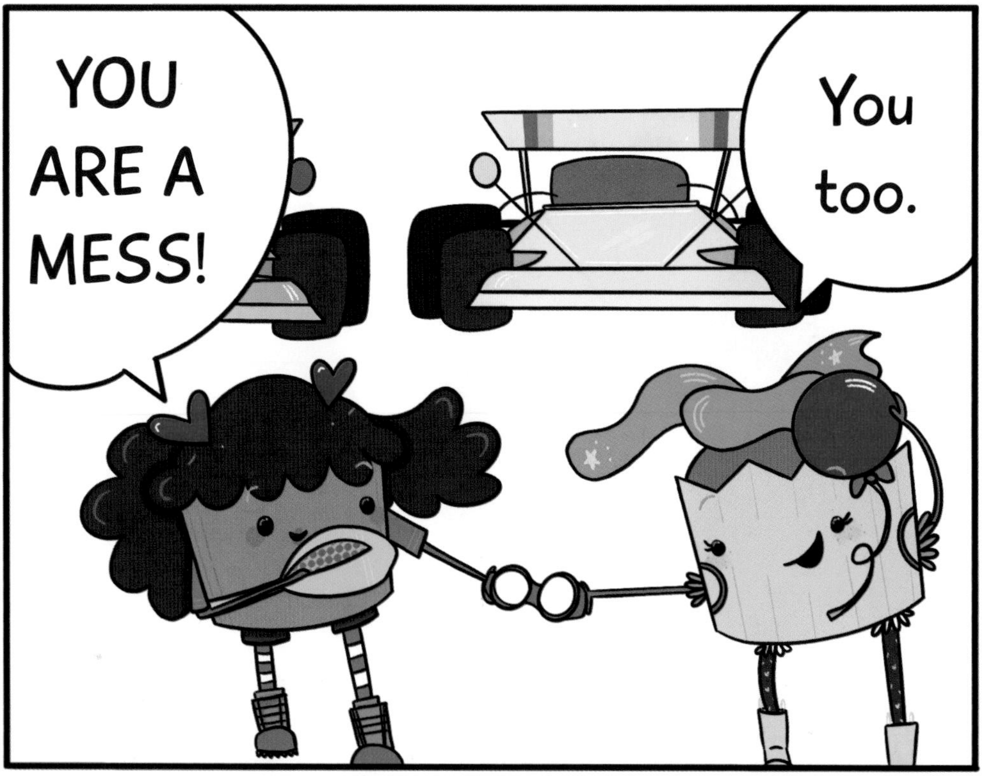
YOU ARE A MESS!
You too.

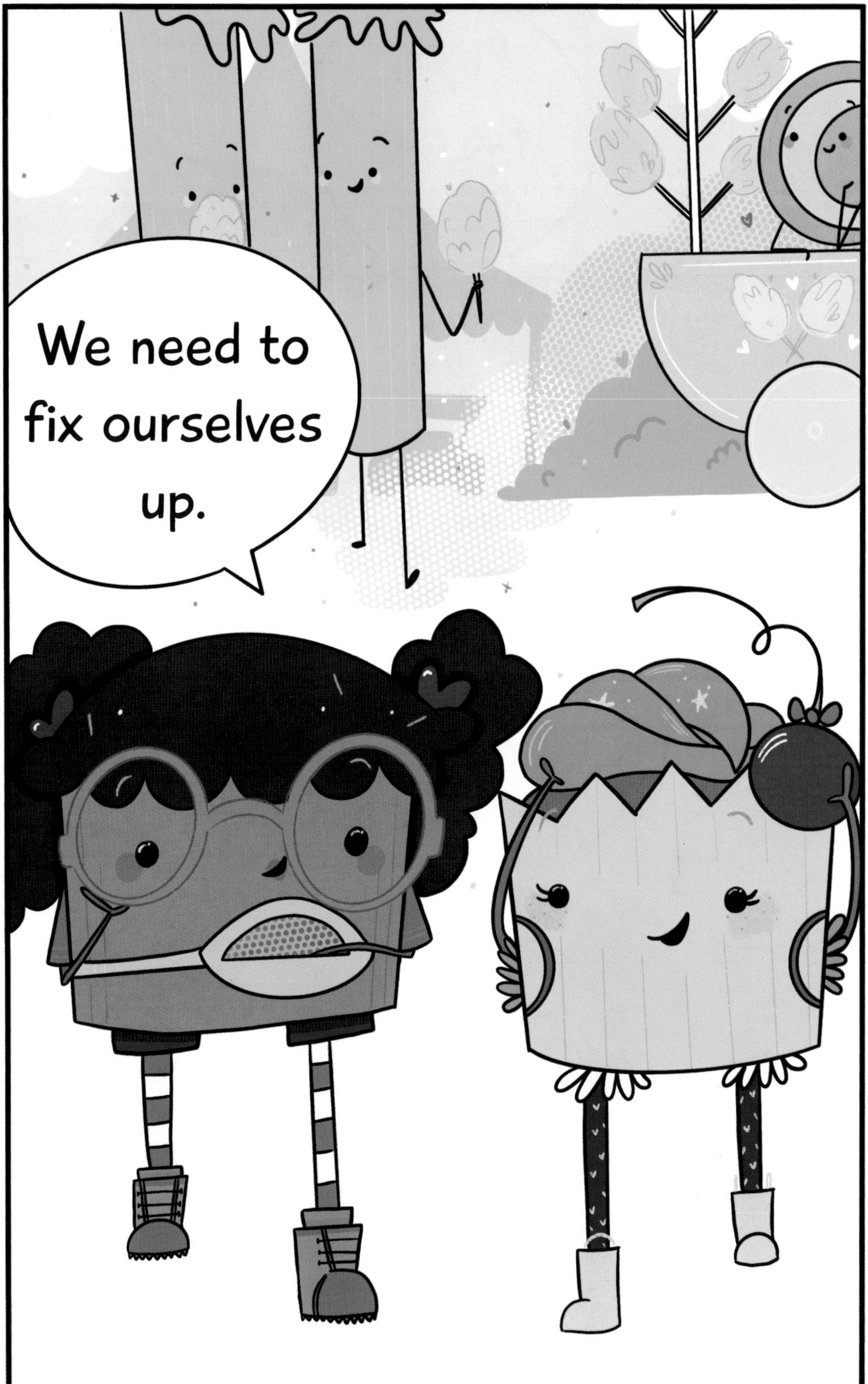
We need to fix ourselves up.

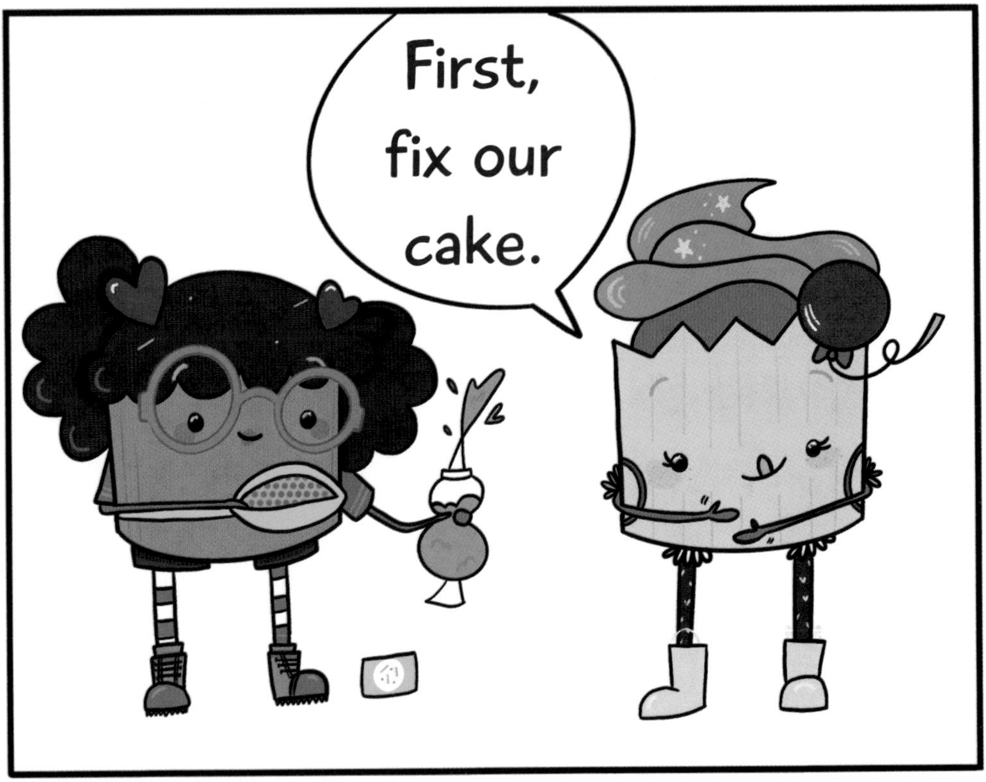
First, fix our cake.

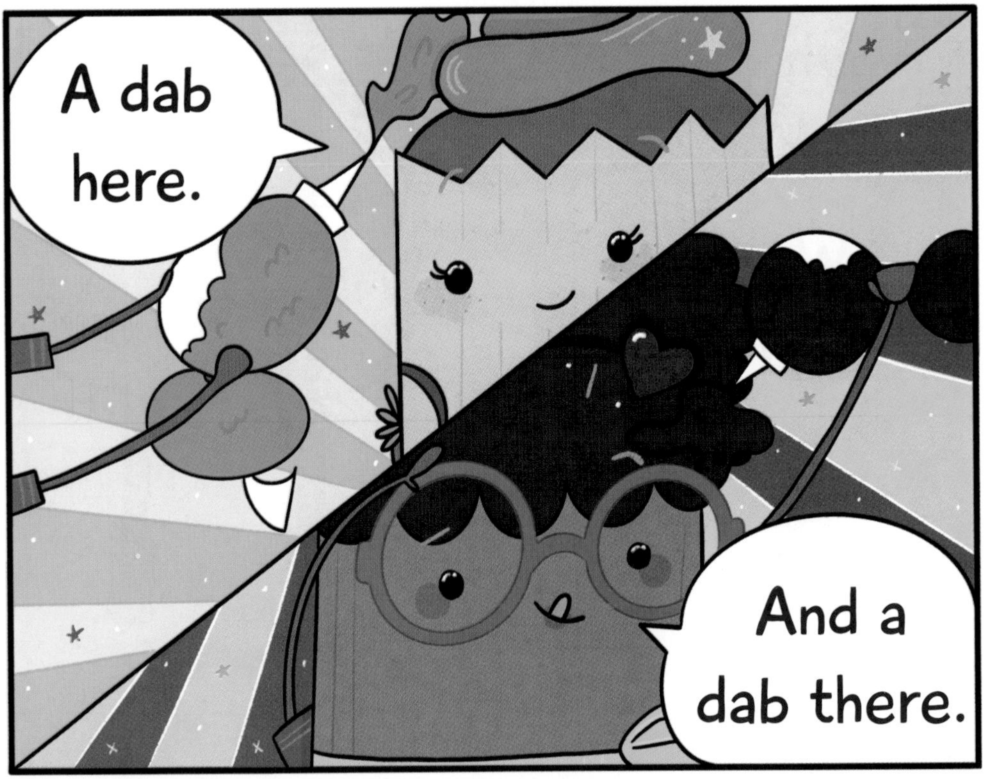
A dab here.
And a dab there.

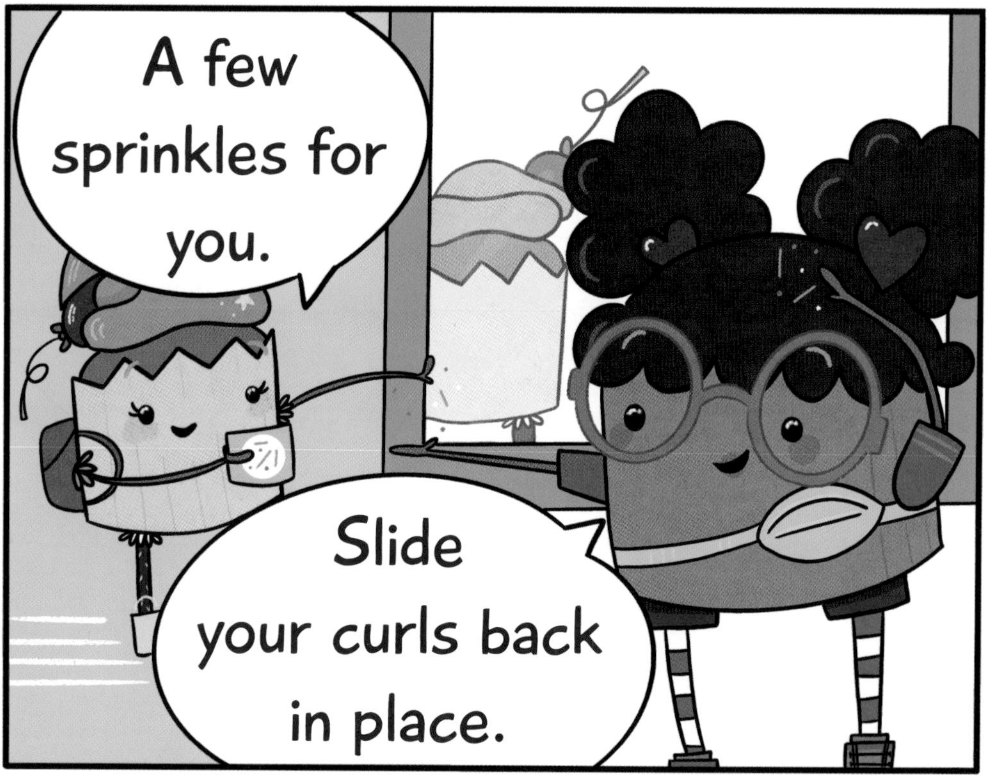
A few sprinkles for you.
Slide your curls back in place.

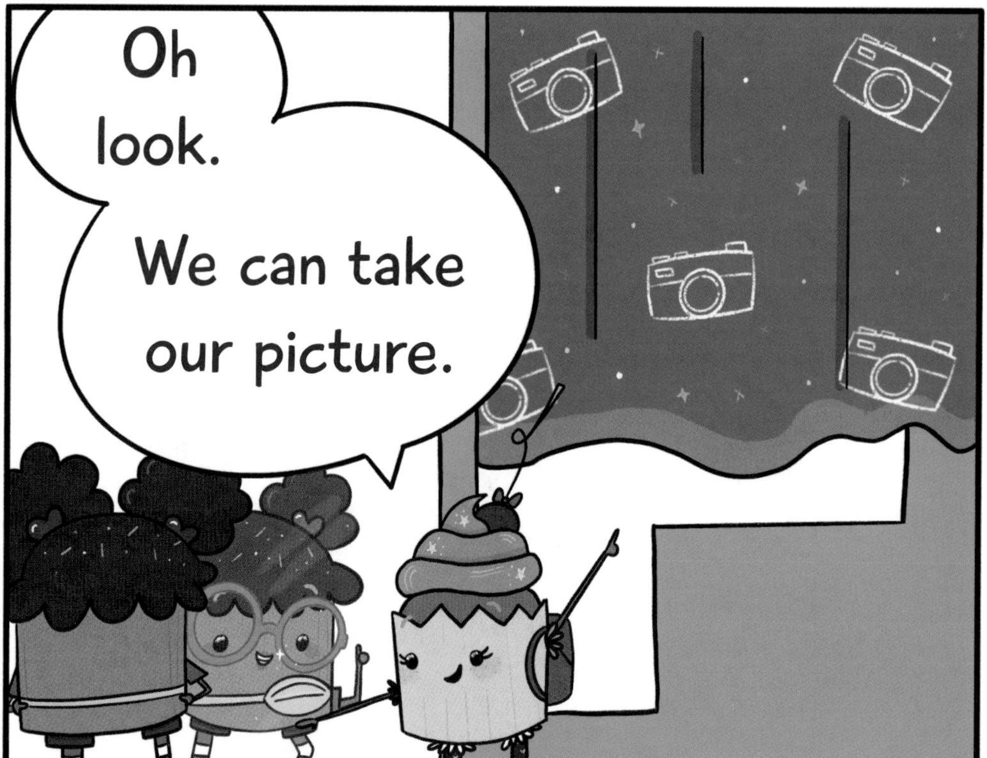
Oh look.
We can take our picture.

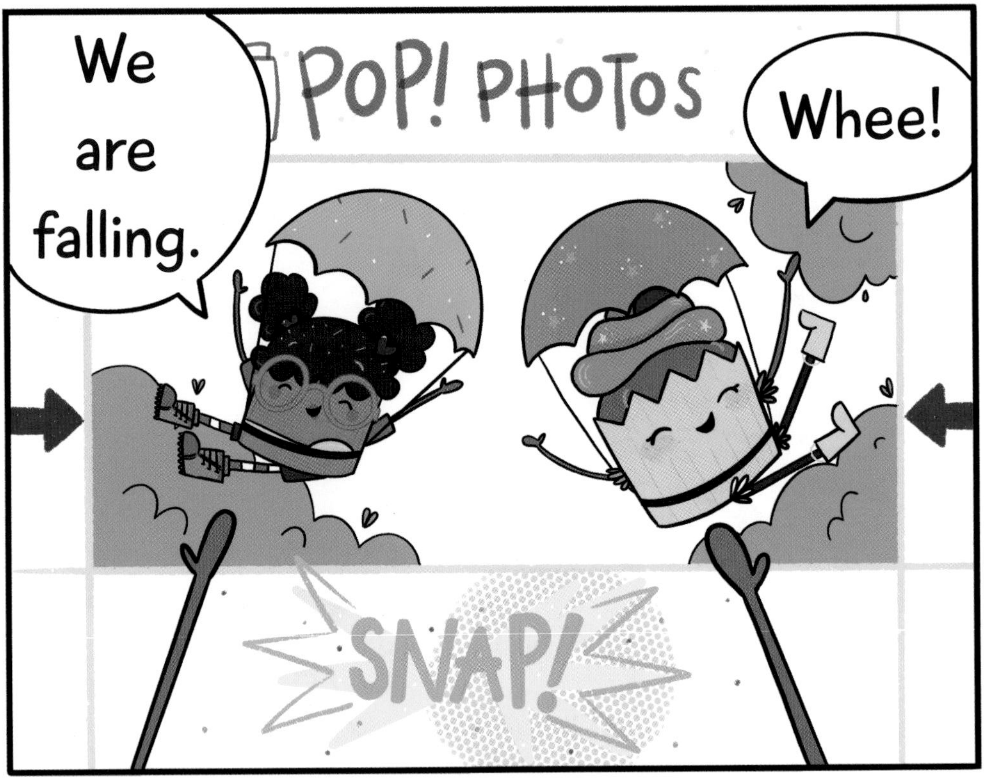
POP! PHOTOS
We are falling.
Whee!
SNAP!

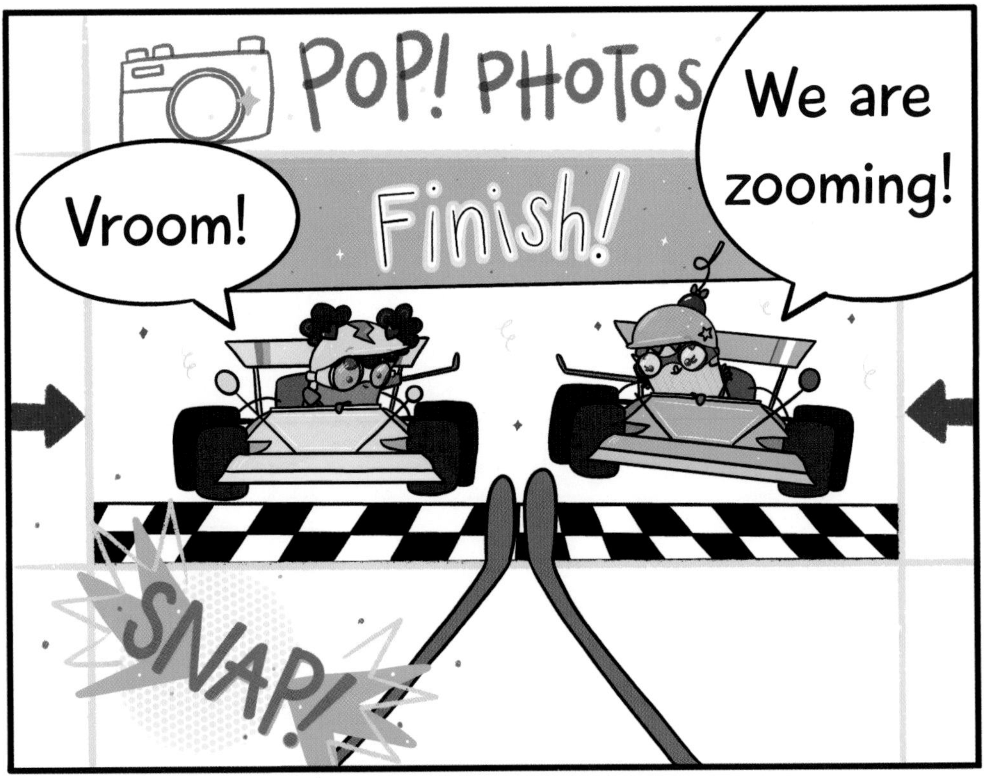
POP! PHOTOS
We are zooming!
Vroom!
Finish!
SNAP!

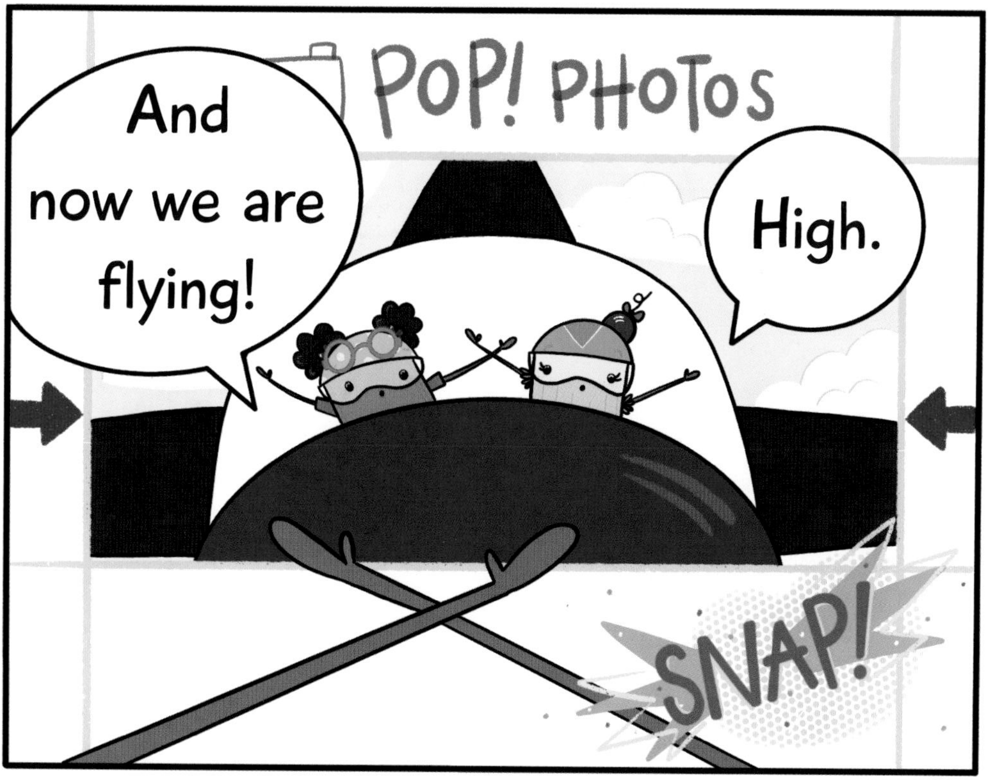
POP! PHOTOS
And now we are flying!
High.
SNAP!

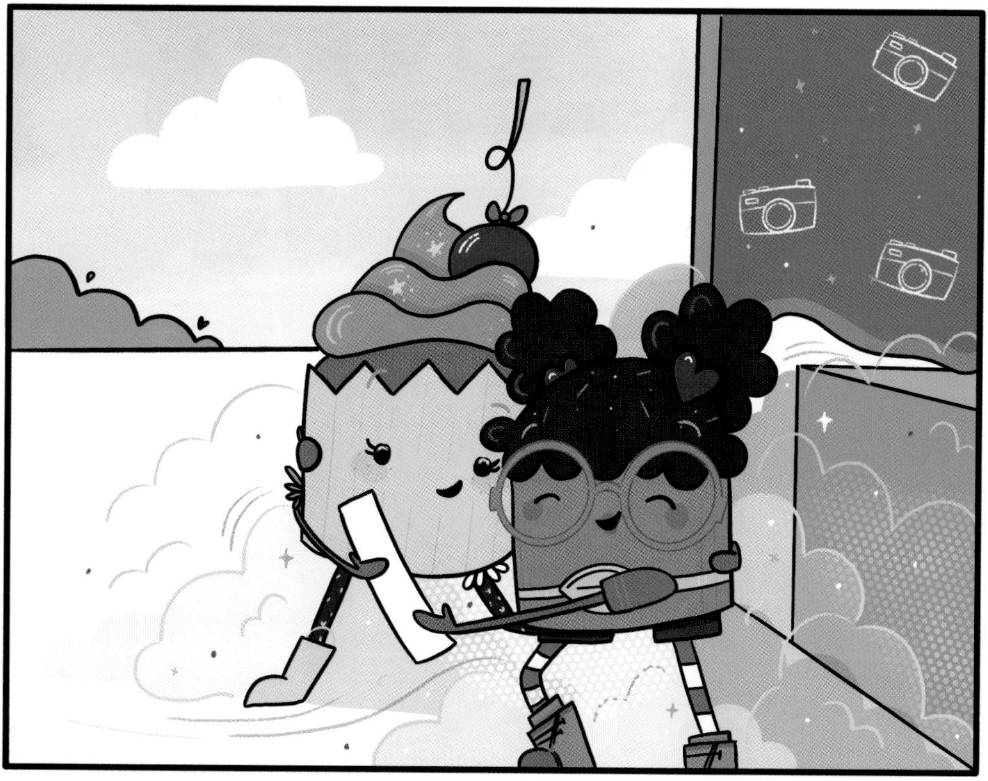

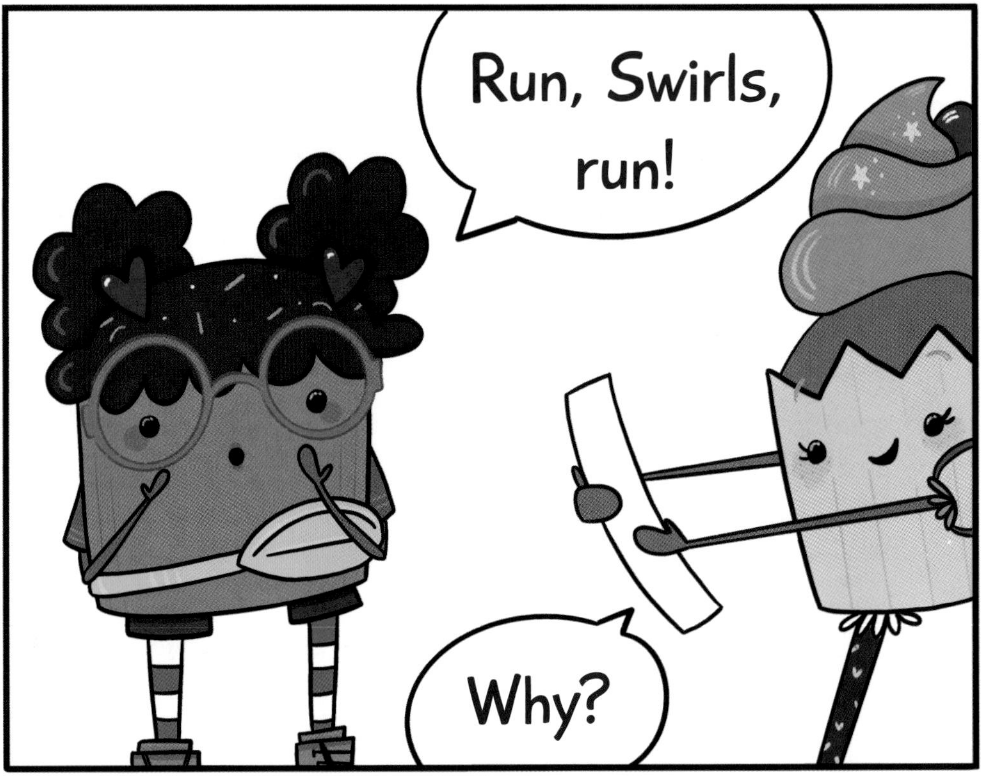
Run, Swirls, run!
Why?

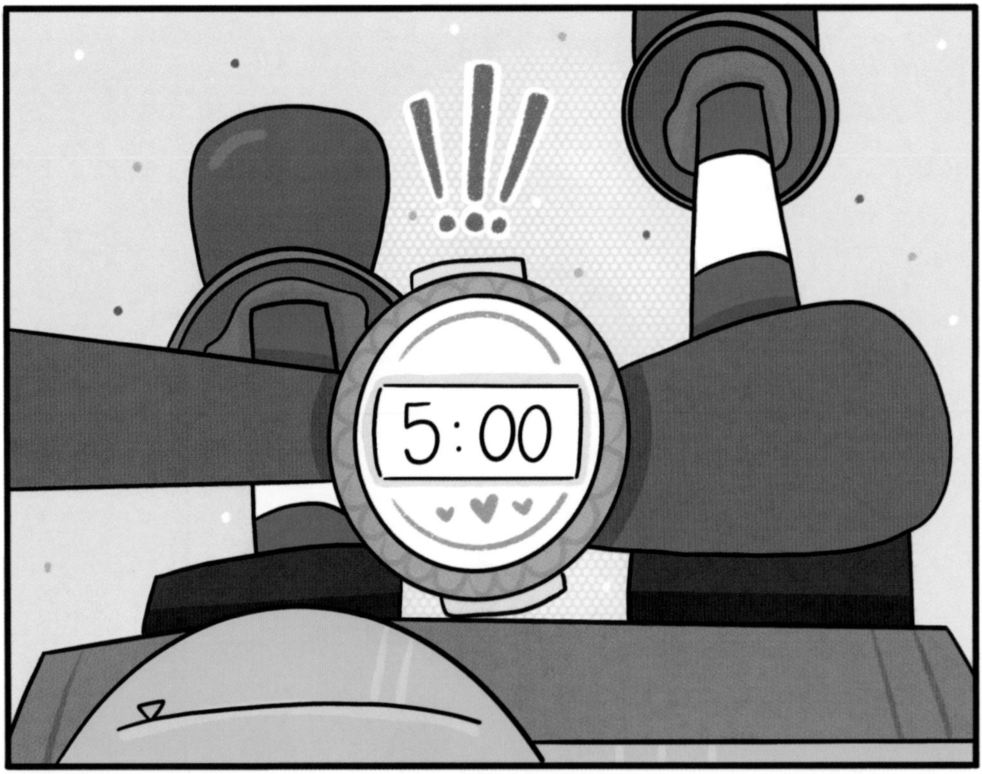
!!!
5:00

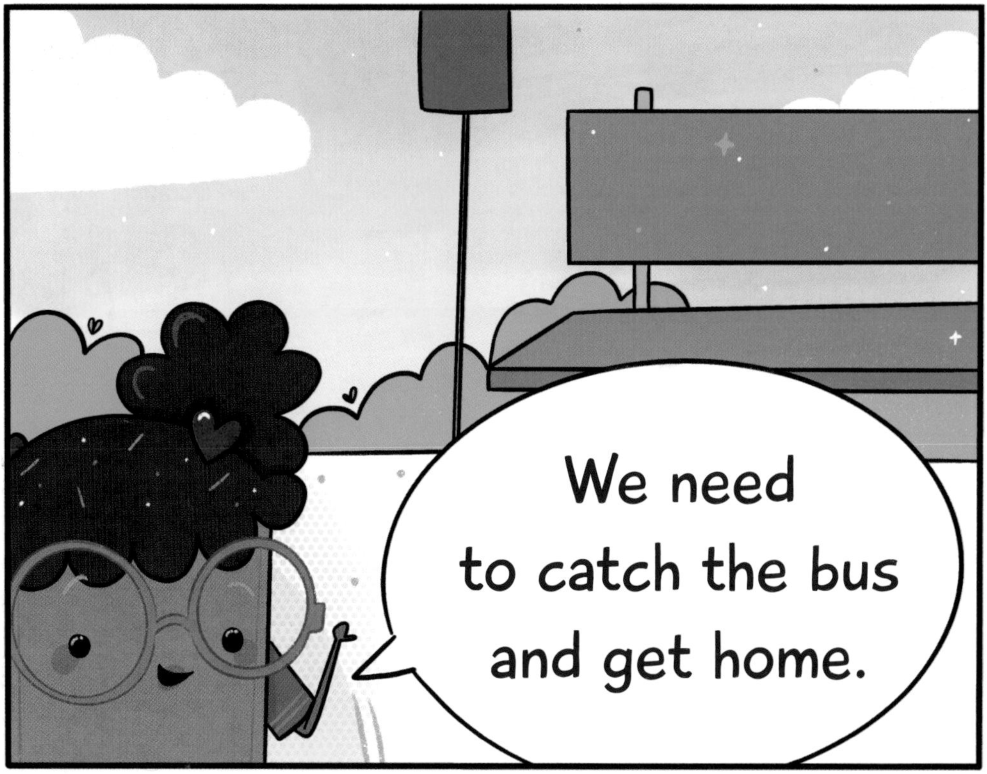
We need to catch the bus and get home.

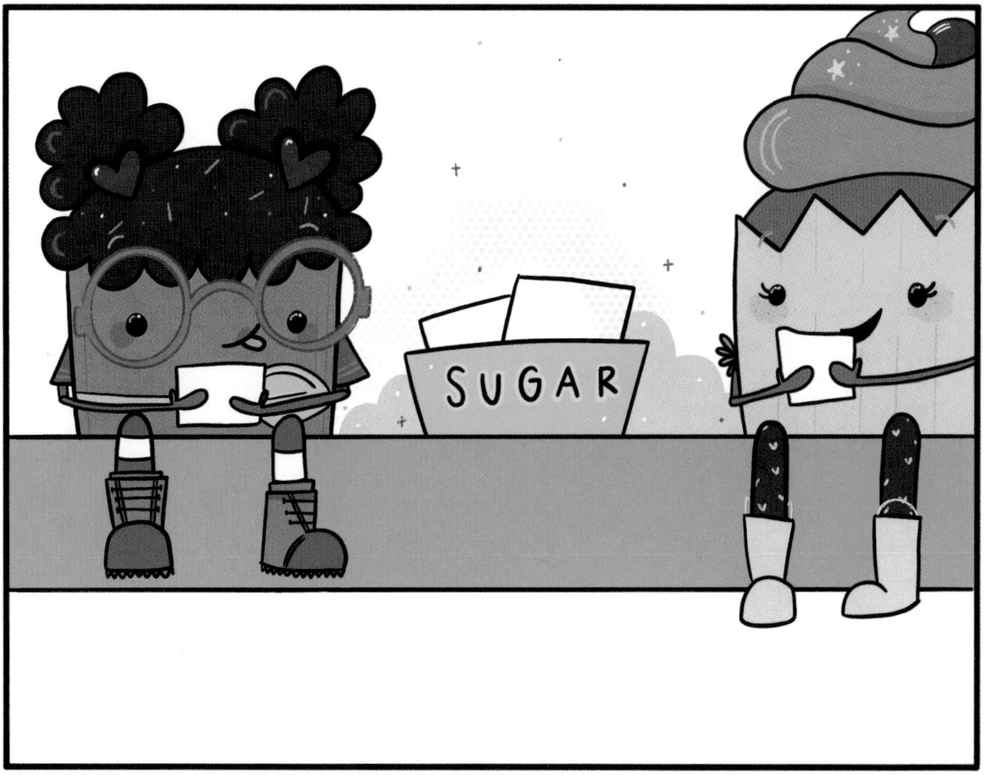
SUGAR

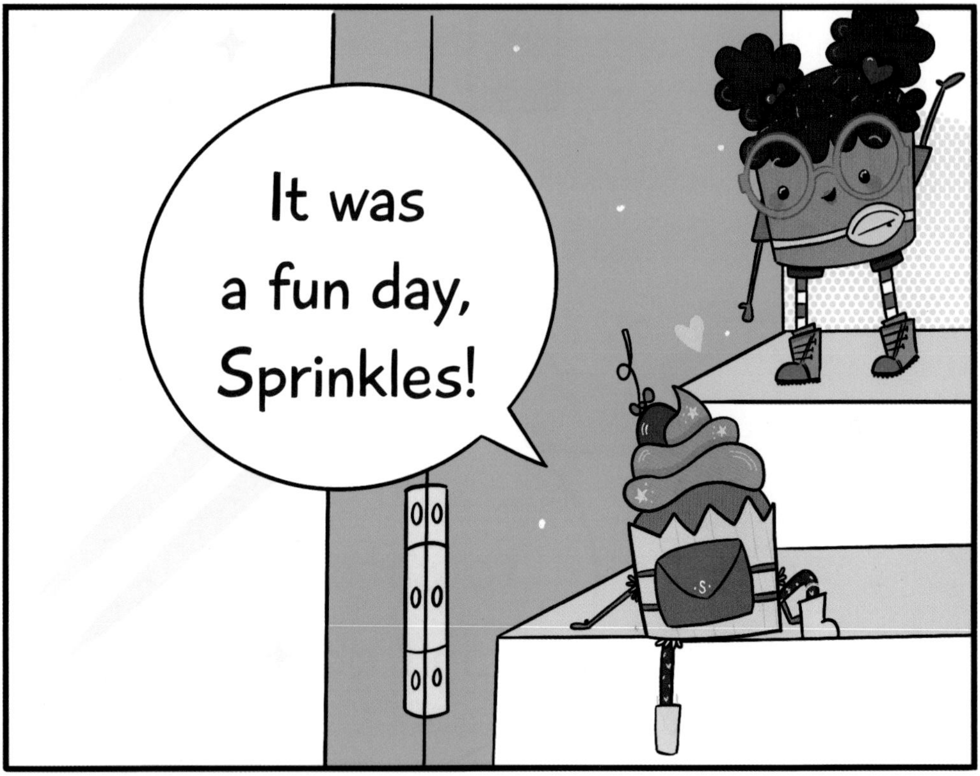
It was a fun day, Sprinkles!

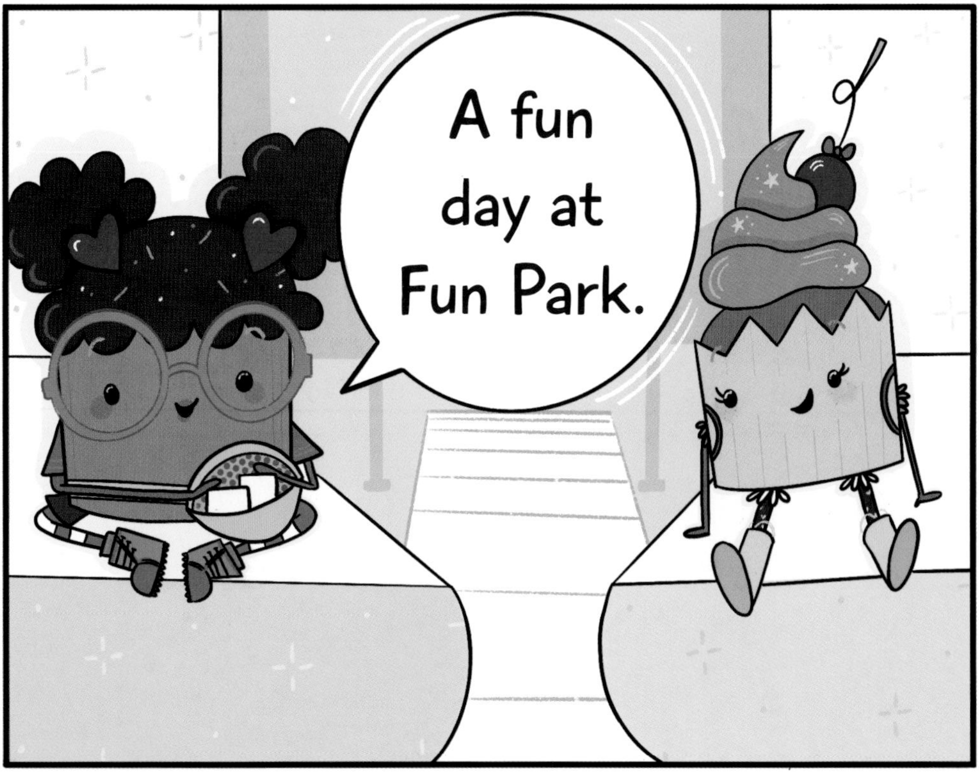
A fun day at Fun Park.

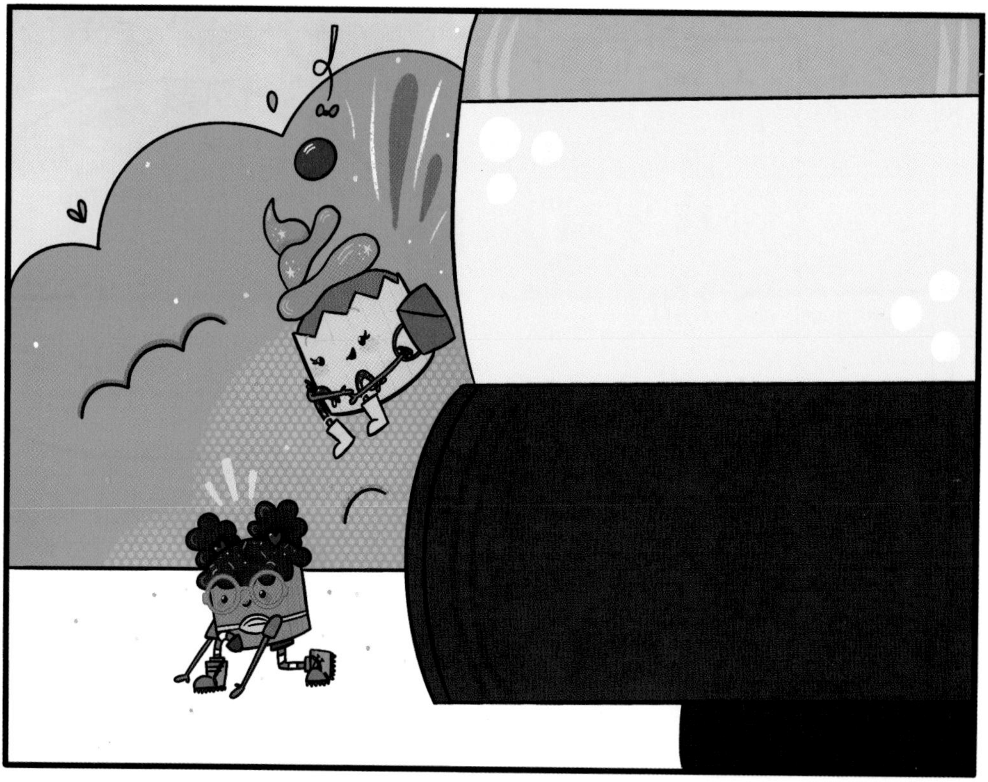

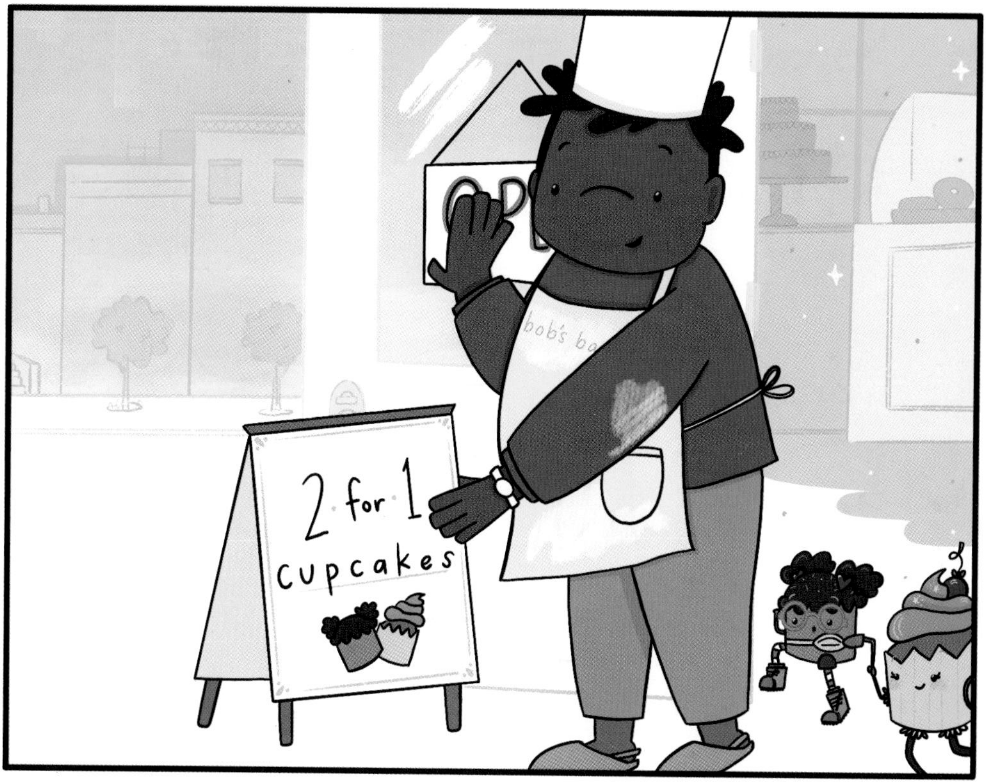
2 for 1
cupcakes

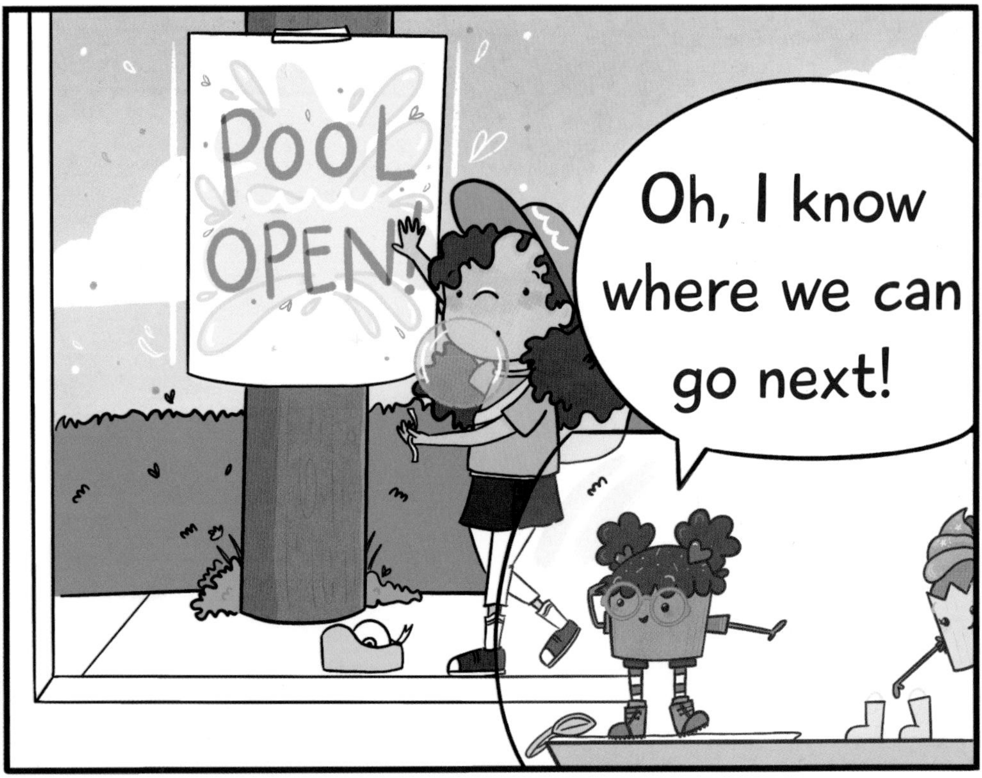
POOL OPEN!
Oh, I know where we can go next!

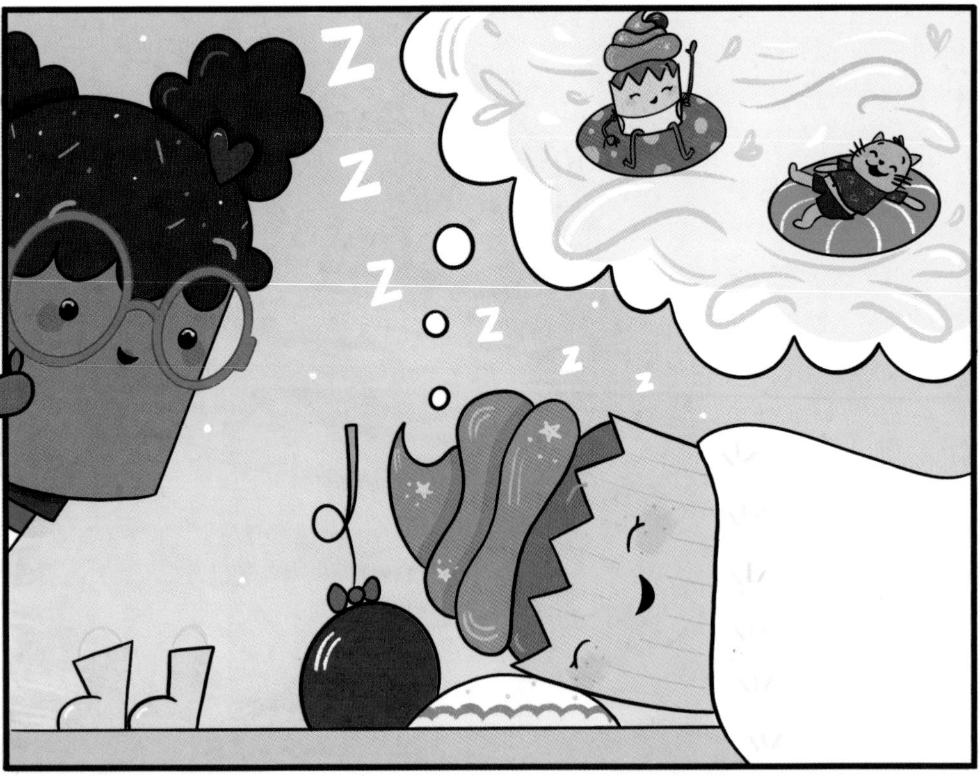
Z Z Z Z Z Z